The
Scarred King

By Amy Horikami

No part of this book may be reproduced in any form whatsoever, whether by graphic, visual, electronic, film, microfilm, tape recording, or any other means, without prior permission of the author.

This work is a work of fiction. The characters, names, incidents, places, and dialogues are products of the author's imagination and are not to be construed as real and are used fictitiously. They are in no way, shape, or form related to any real persons, places, or things and are coincidental if such a case occurs.

Dedication

To my Dad. Thanks for being Stellar! I was a winner when I got you for a Dad!

CHAPTER 1

ROLLAN

I looked out the tall glass window from the third floor of my study. I saw the glamorous carriage approaching, which displayed the sense of wealth only those of high ranking or royalty could afford.

I knew precisely who dwelled inside its carriage walls. Someone probably as puffed up as the carriage itself.

The Princess of Kendall.

I have actually never met the princess before. I made it a point to avoid as many Ladies in and out of my court as possible. I only met with them when forced upon by my Advisor, Jeren, who tried tirelessly to find me a bride. It's not like I was old. I was twenty-eight and still in my prime. My body was well built from the endless hours I spent training with my men. Any woman would be proud of me, that is, if they didn't have to look at my face. Not even the title of King could make a woman look past my appearances. The honor of saving my country did me no good when all you could see were the scars from such a triumph. It seemed the tales of heroes who came home with scars to prove their bravery and sought by many women for their heroic deeds were only that…tales.

I was grateful my men looked past those visible scars. They knew how I received them, many of them having their own scars from those long and dreadful days of battle, but none as visible or brutal as mine. My men were there with me in the heat of those deadly moments, fighting for our lives against our neighboring kingdom to the north, who tried to seize our lands eight years ago. I was a young prince at the time, second in line to the throne, but after that day, I became king after losing not only my father but my brother as well.

I used to feel something when I thought of that day, but after years of shoving down my emotions, I had become hardened, numb to the past that used to torment me. They used to sing songs of glory in the olden days to those warriors who came home from war, victors for their land, but no songs were sung for me. My black heart made me known as the scarred king.

But no matter what they said, they could not deny my kingdom was a fortress that no one dared to try and seize ever again. My men trained harder than most, and while I ruled with an iron fist, my people were safe. But for how long? If I didn't have an heir, it might fall into the wrong hands, which led me to look back out at the carriage approaching. I held back a groan.

I was tired of the endless matches that were made, only to be broken off for some mundane reason. Ladies couldn't look me in the eye without gasps of horror flitting across their features that told me what they really thought of me.

A scar ran down the right side of my face, starting right above my eye and making its way down to the corner of my lip. It would look roguish if it were just a thin line, but it was deformed, with scarred skin formed around the edges.

It didn't matter that the reason I received my scar was heroic. They could never look past that. The reason that haunted me.

Those who did stay, only stayed out of pity. It was never long enough to seal the alliance with marriage, though, but that didn't stop Jeren from trying to shove every available courtier into my castle in hopes that they would see past my scars and hopefully *fix* my broken heart. A heart that I turned to stone.

I had a kingdom to run and would do it with or without a queen by my side. Having an heir could wait a few more years. I wouldn't force any woman to marry me. My men were enough company at the moment with our daily training, and my head housekeeper, Mrs. Warson, did an excellent job keeping the castle in pristine order.

That reminded me of the request King Fredrick sent me in a letter I received a few days ago before their arrival.

He requested that my walls be washed thoroughly for the Princess before she arrived. I thought it was odd and rolled my eyes at his request. Was the princess so afraid to get her hands *dirty* that coming to the Scarred King's Kingdom would ruin her apparel as it brushed against my stone walls?

I ignored the request and almost burnt the letter. Mrs. Warson and my servants were busy enough, and the walls were cleaned regularly. I wouldn't burden them with something so frivolous when it wasn't needed.

I scoffed out loud, just thinking about it as I watched the carriage enter the courtyard. She was almost here. I sighed, preparing myself for what was to come.

I brought my hand up and rubbed the right side of my face, feeling the textured skin that no concoction could ever make smooth again.

I saw the carriage pull around to the large stone steps to the front of my castle, my footmen immediately rushing to open the carriage door.

I sighed and turned away. I didn't need to know what she looked like. They were all the same. Beautiful on the outside but as vain as a peacock on the inside.

She was probably only here because her brother, who had become king recently, forced her to be here.

I reflected on the letter I received a month ago, asking for an alliance between our kingdoms. I was surprised since Fredrick, and I never got along particularly well. In fact, we didn't get along at all, which is probably why he put a clause in the arrangement.

I walked to my desk and pulled the letter out to look over its contents.

...before the alliance is set in stone, I will send my sister, Princess Ellenora, to visit for three months to see if this arrangement is even compatible. If at any time she or I feel that this arrangement will not coincide, I am free to release her from any obligations, and we may withdraw the alliance of marriage, but as such, will keep our kingdoms on friendly terms and continue trading for the benefit of both kingdoms...

I threw it back on the desk. I didn't need three months with the princess to know this wouldn't work. Three seconds would do.

I sat in my chair and leaned back, running my hands through my midnight-black hair in frustration. I kept it a little longer to help cover my scar, but I knew it was useless.

I sighed. *"Why did I have to be born into privilege?"* Maybe when I get old enough, I'll find the closest of kin and bestow the kingdom upon them.

That thought quickly left me when I thought about my uncle and the three sons he had. It was the reason I was still here. They would burn this kingdom to the ground with high taxes, striping my people of everything they had for their greed that couldn't be satiated. I fought too hard and had lost too much to give it up to the greed of that selfish man.

I closed my eyes. A headache was starting to form, and it was only two in the afternoon. Maybe I could use it as an excuse to delay meeting the princess today. I got up to head to my quarters, my cream tunic falling around my hips from being roughly tucked in early. My black pants and dark brown boots were still covered in dirt from the training grounds. I didn't have time to change after my exercise, not that I really wanted to, but maybe if my excuse for having a headache didn't work, I could delay our meeting by changing my clothes into something more suitable.

A knock on the door told me that I was too late in planning my escape, and I held back a groan as my advisor's voice spoke through. It would be just my luck for this to happen.

"Your Majesty, I am here to inform you that-"

The door burst open, and I whipped around to see King Fredrick of Kendall stomping his way into my study with rage in his eyes. My blood boiled at his intrusion. How dare he barge in as if it was his castle and not mine.

Words were at the tip of my tongue, but I didn't have time to release them before he started to berate me.

"Your castle is filthy! Have you no respect for my sister? I have half a mind to take her back to my kingdom and forget this whole foolish idea!" He came up to me, pointing a finger in a scolding manner as if I were a young child who needed to learn a lesson.

I stood tall with my legs apart, arms folded, and glared down at him as he shoved a finger on my chest.

How dare he touch me. He must want a death wish. My eyes went wide, and my blood boiled, but years of training kept me from lashing out at him and ridding him of his finger.

Sadly, I couldn't afford a war over his immature behavior, but he must have seen the threat in my eyes because he stepped back quickly. I didn't miss the glance at my scar, though.

"What do you have to say for yourself?" He sneered.

I stepped towards him, towering over him by a whole foot. He stepped back again, now realizing what a mistake it was to barge in here and reprimand me.

"I'm this close to sending you home, either way, King Fredrick," I spoke in a deadly low tone. "I'm only doing this because you asked *me* to, and if your sister's senses are so fragile, then maybe you should just leave. I don't have time to appeal to such frail creatures when I have a kingdom to run. I'm a king, not a nursemaid."

His face turned beet red, but he didn't say a word as we glared at each other. I glanced at Jeren, who was still frozen in the doorway, wondering what he should do as he looked between us.

"The only reason *I'm* here is because my sister begged me to give you a chance, and the only reason *I'm* staying is to fulfill that promise," he seethed before turning on his heel and stomping out the door.

I watched as he went, but his words surprised me.

He was here because of his sister and not because he wanted to form an alliance of marriage, and was using his sister as a means to get that.

That never happened, and I almost wondered why.

Was barging in here part of some mind game he was trying to play with me? If so, he would regret it. Women never willingly put themselves in my presence. Did she come to see if the rumors were true about the *Scarred King*? A name I hated but was often used among the courts.

"Well, your Majesty…" My advisor spoke up, then cleared his throat as if he didn't know what else to say about what had just happened. Then a look of pity came to his face, and I glared at him to let him know I didn't need it, even though I knew he was one of the few who looked past my scars and truly cared about me as a person.

"It's fine," I waved his worries away. I could technically charge King Fredrick with treason for threatening me, but I would see where this meeting would go, even just to keep Jeren happy. He worked hard as my advisor.

If it went how I thought it would, it would be over by tomorrow, when I sent them away back to Kendall, or fleeing was more likely of how it would go.

"Come, I need a long and hot bath," I told him before making my way out of my study.

"But what about the princess? We don't want to keep them waiting?"

Ever the hostess.

"It will give him time to cool down." Plus, I needed to cool down and mentally prepare myself for rejection. While I told myself it didn't matter, and it didn't, there was some small part of me that was left hollow after each encounter.

Jeren didn't say anything as he followed me to my quarters to help me prepare for the upcoming meeting.

A meeting I dreaded.

CHAPTER 2

ELLEN

"He's selfish, cruel, and had the audacity to not even greet us upon our arrival," my brother paced the floor of the drawing room we had been sent to, his footsteps making it obvious that he was furious.

"How dare he!" He growled out. I knew if I said something, it would make it worse, so I placed a hand on my mother's arm to let her know that she should interfere.

She put her hand on top of mine, letting me know she understood.

"Maybe he didn't realize we were arriving today," my mother's soft voice of reason echoed through the room. As a former queen, her soft words have changed many hearts.

Fredrick scoffed. "As if! He was lounging in his study, which looked over the courtyard. So, don't tell me he didn't know we were coming. He didn't even have the decency to change from his filthy training clothes that were covered in grime and dust."

"That doesn't matter," I called out. Looks meant so little to me, and over the years, it has almost been freeing to look at people's hearts instead of how they dressed.

"It does matter! If he can't respect you in the way I know he should, this arrangement was doomed from the start. In fact, Mother, don't have the servants unpack any trunks yet. I'm going to speak with the coachman and see if we can change horses and head back home, immediately!"

"Now, now," my mother spoke calmly, trying to ease the situation. "It's been a long day of travel, and I'm sure we all just need some rest."

"Rest!" He yelled back, "they didn't even fulfill the simple request of cleaning the walls like I asked. The castle is filthy.

"It's fine," I called out desperately. "I don't care about the walls. It is a simple thing that can be fixed, and Mother will be here to guide me for the time being."

When I was in a new place, I liked to scout the area as much as I could, and using the walls as my guide helped me memorize the layout of the building. That way, I could have more independence and not solely rely on others to help me consistently. I wasn't a cripple, and I wouldn't let my condition be an excuse not to try and live a normal life to the fullest.

"No. He has no respect for you already. I will not have my sister living here for three months, enduring this barbarian, because that is exactly what he is."

I was worried he would make due on his threat, but I prayed he was just taking this moment to let out his frustrations and would soon be rational after he calmed down.

"We don't know that. You can't judge a person within the first few minutes of meeting them. Give him a chance. Did he even know about me and the reason the walls needed to be cleaned?"

Not that it mattered if the walls were clean or not, I was just glad I had made it this far in actually getting here when I thought it would never happen.

He didn't respond, and that was answer enough.

"Why didn't you mention it?"

"I...I thought I did, but..."

I took a deep breath. I was used to this. My brother was continually trying to protect me, and I felt he was more afraid of protecting my feelings than I was. Even though I often told him that I had accepted my fate. There was no use in living with regrets when you couldn't change it.

So, I accepted what had happened to me and tried to make the best out of it; even if others reacted negatively, I wasn't going to let that bring me down; even if that *other* person was the man I wanted to marry, and because of my brother's folly, I might not even get a chance, but there was still hope.

We still were meeting with him.

Ever since I asked, no, begged him to form an alliance with the Kingdom of Maren, he's been trying to talk me out of it.

Ever since I heard of the *scarred king*, I felt drawn to him in a way that was unexplainable, which was odd. I've never been drawn to people before. I usually kept to myself and inside my castle walls. I wondered at first if it was just out of curiosity or a chance for a new adventure, but deep down, I knew it was something more.

He grabbed my hands. "Please, Ellen, don't do this. I can't bear to leave you here all by yourself. Not with that monster."

"She won't be here by herself," my mother chimed in. "I'm staying, or have you forgotten."

He released my hands and stood up. "No, but it's not enough, and I don't know why you are being so agreeable to this, Mother. Did you not just hear what had happened?"

"Why? Do you think I would put my own daughter in danger?" Mother asked with a tone that dared him to defy her, and we knew her patience was running thin.

"No," he spoke softly, and I smiled. No one could challenge a queen, even a former one, but mostly if that queen was your mother.

"Good. It's settled, then. No more talking about it," my mother's cheery voice filled the air, leaving no room for argument.

Fredrick huffed, and I almost laughed. He was so dramatic, but he was also loyal to a fault. I loved and cared for him and knew our kingdom was in great hands.

"So, when did he say he was going to meet us?" I asked, trying to keep the eagerness out of my voice.

"I don't know." I could hear the worry as he paced the floor, and then the door creaked open, letting me know that someone was coming in.

My body froze, and I faced the door from where the sound came. I held my breath, anticipating the King of Maren to step in, wondering what his reaction would be when he saw me.

"Ah, tea!" My mother exclaimed for me, knowing I thought it was someone else. I was grateful she was always in tune with me and my thoughts.

A tinge of disappointment swept through me. I didn't have an appetite at the moment. I was too nervous to meet King Rollan. I wondered what he would think of me.

While I knew I wasn't flashy and in the latest style, most ladies of the court wore, since practicality was more my taste. I had Mother help me order some beautiful, elegant gowns for this meeting. My golden hair was up in a loose chignon, along with curls that framed my face.

I reached up and lightly touched them to see if they were still holding their shape and was glad to feel they were.

"Come, Ellen, drink some tea. It's herbal and will soothe your stomach."

She always knew what I needed, even before I did.

"I'm fine for the moment," I told her, but she grabbed my hand and opened my palm to place a teacup inside of it.

"Now, now, I don't need two children with whom I need to see reason. There's only so much patience a mother has."

I felt her shift next to me, "you, too, Fredrick." She told my brother, and the slurping sound made me chuckle that Mother was forcing him to drink tea with us.

I smiled and shifted my hand, feeling for the handle of the teacup before bringing it to my mouth.

Right before I took a sip, a knock on the door filled my ears, and I paused. I figured it was either another servant coming to ask if we needed anything, show us our rooms, or someone announcing the King was coming.

"Come in," my mother called out, and the door creaked, letting me know it was being opened.

My mother stiffened next to me, and it made me lower the cup from my mouth, wondering what was wrong, "Is everything-" but then it dawned on me as mother suddenly stood up.

"Your Majesty, it is a privilege to finally meet you."

I stiffened as panic coursed through me. I tried to set the teacup down but was struggling to find where the table was, so instead, I stood up with the teacup in hand and gave a slight curtsey in place, knowing I probably looked foolish.

"Your Majesty," I spoke with the voice of forced confidence, even though embarrassment coursed through me.

I used my mother's queue of sitting to finally sit as well, and when I didn't hear my brother give his respects, I slowly put my foot forward until I felt his foot and slightly kicked his boot.

He grumbled something that sounded like " *Your Majesty,* " but I wasn't quite sure. He didn't even stand, and I figured that was the best I was going to get, but prayed our rooms tonight wouldn't be in the dungeon with metal bars for company due to his disrespect.

Suddenly, my body responded to a heated gaze that I could feel was watching me, and all thoughts of the dungeon left my mind, and I instinctively put my head down. This was the moment I had been waiting and dreading for the past few months. What must he think of me? I couldn't dare bring my gaze to him for fear of his judgment, especially since my brother didn't make him aware of my condition.

"I would like to speak with the Princess alone," his deep voice filled my soul and sent butterflies swirling in my stomach. I pushed that down, wondering why he was affecting me so. It's not like I have never met another man before, but he wasn't just any man.

If this all worked out, he would be my betrothed and then my husband. That is, if he could look past my weaknesses and see my strengths, just like my mother did.

That gave me the courage I needed. I would not cower before a king. I would show him I was his equal. I would prove to him that we were one and the same and that I could be a valuable asset to his kingdom.

If only he would give me a chance.

I lifted my head high, and the slight intake of air was all I needed to know that he finally saw me for what I was.

I forced myself to keep my head up because that's not all I was. I was so much more, and I would show him that.

I was more than this.

I was more than just blind.

CHAPTER 3

ROLLAN

When I first entered the room and saw her stumbling to place her teacup on the table, I thought it was nerves. I grew irritated that my very presence made the most beautiful young woman I had ever seen tremble before me. Her golden hair was pinned up in a loose bun, and she wore a light blue dress that was simple but elegant in style and only enhanced her beauty.

I scolded myself for gawking at her. She didn't even have the decency to look me straight in the eye when her mother welcomed me into the room.

I watched her as her mother invited me to sit down, but I didn't move.

"Well, as I was saying..." she kept going, but I didn't hear a word because at that very moment, the princess lifted her head up and looked at me. Her shoulders squared with courage, and I wondered what she would think of me, of my scars, once her gaze reached my face. Was I so hideous that she had to look like she was preparing for battle?

I forced myself to stay still, not showing any sign of nervousness that seemed to course through me. I didn't know why I cared so much. It's been a while since I cared about what a woman has thought of me. I noticed her eyes were a light blue and not quite focused on me, only looking in my general direction. Was I so revolting that she couldn't look me straight in the eye?

Who was I kidding? I knew I was. I've seen myself plenty of times. I, too, would be frightened, but for some reason, I wanted her to look past that, to see me for who I truly was.

Which was honestly a puzzle since I didn't know myself. I've hidden behind a mask for so long that I didn't know how to be anything but cruel and indifferent.

She still didn't look at me directly, and my anger started to grow as I tried to focus on her eyes, to catch just a glimpse, and to force her to make eye contact.

Then it dawned on me, like a punch to my gut as I continued to watch her. Things were all starting to make sense.

Princess Ellenora of Kendall was blind.

Rage filled me. Was this some sick joke?

"What is the meaning of this!" I called out, interrupting the former Queen of Kendall and whatever she was rambling on about.

"Um, what do you mean, your Majesty?" she asked innocently enough, but I knew better.

"Is this some joke to you!" I laughed out of anger, "I don't have time for this. Who put you up to this," I turned to King Fredrick, demanding an explanation. He stood up, the same fury in his eyes as he stood before his sister, protecting her from my view.

If it even *was* his sister.

How come I didn't know the Princess of Kendall was blind?

Surely, that would have been public information.

"I knew we should never have come," Fedrick snarled. Death was in his eyes and a possessiveness I'd never seen before as he stood before his sister.

"Joke? I assure you, that *this* is not some joke," the queen responded with confusion.

"You think only a blind girl could love me? Am I so ugly that you had to waste your time to make a fool out of me? But you're the real fool here! Where is the real princess?" I demanded, but I knew the answer and what a buffoon I was making myself out to be. It seemed all my self-control went out the window, and I couldn't reel myself in.

Right then, the beautiful girl stood up. Her cheeks either flamed with rage or embarrassment, but she held her composure while I lost mine.

"I *am* the real princess," her voice quaked with passion but was firm nonetheless, "and the only ugly thing in this room is your heart. I may not see like you do, but I see you very clearly from how you have treated me and my family in the last ten seconds since you entered the room. The only fool here is you, your Majesty!"

Then she sat back down on the settee and turned away from me, her hands firmly clasped in her lap, but I noticed they were shaking. Then she faced me once more, her face red with rage.

"I was going to give you the benefit of the doubt from what my brother has said, but it seems to me his words were highly understated."

She looked away once more, turning so she almost faced the other direction, her whole body shaking with emotion.

I didn't miss the tear that slipped down her cheek, and my heart clenched, and I immediately regretted everything I had done.

I didn't know what to say, and for the first time in a long time, shame filled me from her words.

She was right. I was a fool. So, I did what I always did.

I ran.

CHAPTER 4

ELLEN

That could not have gone any worse, and I couldn't believe the words that spilled out of my mouth to his majesty, but my pride got the better of me.

I closed my eyes, trying to keep the tears from spilling over, but I failed miserably. I heard footsteps leave the room, and I prayed it was King Rollan's. I don't think I ever have been so bold in my life, but to accuse me of coming here as a joke, crossed the line for me. My heart was breaking at his cruel words.

"I told you! We are leaving immediately," my brother called out.

Mother placed her hand on my arm, "I'm so sorry, dear. I didn't think he would act like that, but maybe your brother is right. This is a lost cause, and it's best if we head back to our kingdom."

I gathered my emotions, feeling so foolish. Maybe she was right, but deep down, I didn't want to leave. But if that's how our first encounter went, who was to say there was any hope for the future? Even though logic said to go, my heart was still telling me to stay, but I brushed it off.

"Maybe you are right," I sighed, feeling defeated.

I heard my brother's footsteps stop right before me, then felt his touch as he grabbed my hands, "Ellen, you have the purest heart I know. You give without expecting anything in return, but I can't let that…that monster ruin all that is good in you," his voice soft and full of concern.

I reached out my hand until I touched his arm, "I know, but aren't we all a little broken inside? Don't we all have ugly parts of us we wish to hide? Some are just more visible than others. If I have learned anything from the accident that happened to me so long ago, it is that looks can be deceiving. I truly get to know people by their hearts, and for some reason, I know there is some good in him."

"Ellen," Fredrick said desperately, "I know you always look for the good in people, and it's a valuable trait, but that man is too far gone. Nothing can redeem him from what he just did, what he said. Sometimes we must see a lost cause for what it is…lost."

I sighed. Maybe he was right.

"Well, since we are here, let us stay for the ball and then return home," Mother interrupted while patting my arm. "Then we can give our horses some time to rest before making the long journey back."

Her response sounded logical, but I wondered if she had an alternative motive.

"I can hire new horses, Mother. I don't want to be in this castle a second longer," Fredrick interjected.

"Well, what does Ellen want to do?" Mother asked. "She is the reason we are here, after all.

I didn't answer because I didn't know. The King thought I was some joke brought here to make fun of him. It hurt deeply that he thought so. I thought that maybe he would look past my eyesight and see me for who I really was, like how he probably wanted others to see him, but I was a fool.

"I don't know," I offered after a few minutes of silence.

"Well, I know. We are leaving," Fredrick stated.

"Now, Fredrick," Mother spoke sternly. "While I know you rule our kingdom with a just heart and mind, I think we should let Ellen decide what to do in this particular matter."

I heard him scoff, and I could only imagine the eye roll he held back from our Mother.

I quickly thought about it since I knew they expected an answer. I was tired after the long trip, and it would be nice to rest for a few days, even if nothing came out of the trip. The thought of returning to the carriage after a long journey made my muscles ache. But deep down, I knew the truth of why I wanted to stay, resting being my excuse. The ball was two days away, a gesture to welcome our alliance and hopefully a betrothal. I would do all that I could to make sure the king saw me in a different light. Who knew, maybe things could change. Maybe he could see that I wasn't just some princess who needed someone to continually look after her. I was as independent as someone who could see. Mother raised me that way. I wasn't an invalid, and I would prove that to him. I just wish I had more time than only two days to prove I was capable. It seemed it would take a lot of convincing for him after what I had just heard.

"I think Mother is right. Let us stay for the ball. We can rest, and then if things haven't improved, we can go home."

"They won't improve," Fredrick mumbled, frustrated under his breath, but Mother cut him off.

"I think that's a wonderful idea, darling," her voice was overly optimistic, which I needed.

"Three days, that's it," my brother's voice gave no room for argument, "then we are gone. I don't care what happens; I will not have you stay any longer than necessary with that monster."

I sighed and nodded my head, wondering how I was going to change the heart of a *monster* in three days to see me as someone who was equal to him.

I stood up and thought I might as well get started now, and it was looking like I wouldn't be getting any rest after all.

CHAPTER 5

ELLEN

I woke up early the following day with such determination that I felt I could conquer the world.

I had my maid, Sophia, pick out a dress and style my hair with lots of curls, then pin it in a half-up style with a braided crown. I had to look the part of queen if I was ever going to convince the King of Maren that I was worthy to rule by his side.

I also needed to study the castle so I could eventually get around all by myself without assistance, as I did in my castle back in Kendall.

"Sophia, if you could grab my walking stick," I told my handmaiden.

She handed me the long, skinny staff that was beautifully carved with intricate designs of leaves and gems throughout the wood.

"Today, I need you to guide me around the castle until I become familiar with it."

"Yes, princess," she told me with a tone that hinted at a smile.

Sophia has been with me for years, and I trusted her completely. She was one of the few who gave me the space I needed to flourish and didn't hover over me like some of the others did.

"Princess?" Sophia enquired after I stood up, with the staff in my hand

"Yes?" I turned toward the general direction of her voice.

"I was thinking, since we are new to this place, that it might be beneficial for you to have a castle guide that would know the rooms and allow you to memorize the layout faster, but I will still be by your side the entire time."

This was another reason I loved her. While she knew my desire for independence, she was also proficient.

"That would be wonderful. Thank you, Sophia."

"It is my honor, your highness. I will grab a servant and be back soon."

I heard her muffled footsteps and the door close behind her.

I took a deep breath now that I was alone in the room and decided to walk around to review the layout, even though I memorized it last night when they showed me to my quarters. I counted my steps back to the bed until I hit the wooden leg. I smiled. Seventeen steps was exactly what I knew it would be.

While I was blind, I didn't see complete darkness as most people thought. I could see light, but it was blurry to no end, and the spectacles they gave me brought no improvement. The way I described it to the many healers who tried to help me was that all I could see were blurry blobs as if I was looking through a fogged-up window. I could see some color, but nothing more, and it was only a tiny window in my vision, that was surrounded by a dark blur.

I turned back around and slightly adjusted my angle, and counted twenty steps to the settee that was placed before the fire, but when I didn't reach it. I took one more step and hit it with my walking staff.

I mentally took notes and started to form a picture of the room in my mind as I continued going over the layout until Sophia came back.

After ten minutes, I heard a knock on the door, and told them to enter.

"I'm sorry to keep you waiting, your Highness, but all the servants were busy."

"It's okay. We shall do just fine on our own," I told her, not wanting her to feel bad since she always tried so hard to please me.

"Which is why I offered to show you the castle."

I stopped moving when I heard the male voice that I wasn't familiar with.

Heavy footsteps entered the room, and I turned towards the sound, seeing a blurry vision of blue.

"My name is Lord Jeren, and I am King Rollan's advisor."

I gave a slight bow of my head towards his voice, surprised King Rollan's advisor offered to show us around, surely, he must be busier than the servants, which made me wonder what King Rollan was up to. Did he want a report about me? To prove to others that I truly was not up for the tasks as queen.

Those thoughts made me stand a little bit taller. I would prove my worth to King Rollan, even if it were through his advisor. I would not leave this Kingdom with my head hung low in shame of who I was. I was the Princess of Kendall, and I knew my worth.

"How kind of you, Lord Jeren. I'm sure your schedule is busy, so please don't feel obligated. I will do just fine with my handmaiden."

"Oh, please, your highness, I insist. I would love to show you around, and then you can ask any questions you may have, and I would be delighted to answer them."

I smiled. This man seemed nice. So, different from his King, but I reminded myself that first impressions rarely showed people's true motives. Even if they did yell at you and call you a joke. That thought stung my heart, but I didn't let it show.

"That would be wonderful. Maybe we'll bump into His Majesty along the way, and he can join us on our tour?" I asked, trying not to sound too desperate. Maybe he would see for himself that I was not incompetent.

There was silence for a few seconds, and I knew I should not have said anything, but I only had three days until the ball, and I had to start somewhere. Otherwise, I would be gone, and the three months of seeing if this would work, would never happen.

"Well...his majesty is held up at the moment," his voice full of regret, but the last part he spoke with enthusiasm, "but do not fret, I'm sure we'll see him."

I held in a sigh and smiled, trying not to feel defeated. It seemed Lord Jeren was not opposed to us bumping into His Majesty, or he was trying to appease me and spare my feelings. Time soon would tell.

But I didn't have time.

"I understand. He is a busy man."

Then I told him how I would like to learn the castle layout and what I needed to do to accomplish that.

"Understood, which is why I had the castle walls cleaned last night."

I smiled at his thoughtfulness. "Thank you, that was unnecessary, but I am grateful."

I liked to run my hand along the walls to guide me, along with my walking staff in places that I did not know. It helped me feel grounded when everything around me was blurry.

"Shall we begin," I smiled.

"Yes, if you'll follow me," Lord Jeren responded, and I could hear his footsteps retreating.

I felt the presence of Sophia by my side, "I'll be right here, princess," she whispered just for my ears.

She led me to the door while I counted the rest of my steps, then moved my hand directly to the wall. She stepped away from my side, giving me the independence I needed, while still being close. Soon, I wouldn't need the walls as my guide once I learned the castle layout well enough.

I started to walk and count my steps while Lord Jeren pointed out rooms as I ran my hand over their door frames. Sophia told me how many doors were in each hallway and warned me ahead of time about end tables so I wouldn't accidentally bump into them and embarrass myself.

We made our way around almost the entire castle, and still, we did not stumble upon the king.

"Is the King not inside today? I was hoping we would bump into him."

"His duties have called him outside the castle, but," then he paused, "would you like to walk the gardens? They are beautiful this time of year. The flowers are in bloom, and the colors are…well…maybe not since…"

I laughed to ease the advisor's fumble. I knew it was hard sometimes when people first met me and wanted to show me things, only to realize their ideas did not quite work when I could not see.

"Yes, that would be lovely," I smiled, "I love walking the gardens and smelling the beautiful aroma around me. Maybe you could describe the flowers to me, Lord Jeren, and I'll have a glorious vision in my mind of your castle gardens."

I heard him release a breath. "Yes, that sounds like a splendid idea."

I reached out my hand to signal Sophia to grab it. It let her know that I was done counting and memorizing and would enjoy this time in the gardens.

She hooked her arm through mine, and off we went.

The moment we stepped through the castle doors, I felt the sun on my skin. A slight wind blew my hair back from my face, making me feel free.

My brother was so strict about my movements back in Kendall that I almost felt like a prisoner in my own home. I knew he did it because he loved me and was worried about anything happening to me, but here, he didn't have as much control over me as he did back home. The reason being I made it part of our deal before we left that he would allow me more freedom to spend time with King Rollan. While the deal wasn't strictly being upheld, I'd take any liberty granted me, even if it was to roam the gardens with His Majesty's advisor.

Lord Jeren took us down a path and described every flower in detail to me so that I could almost visualize the entire garden in my mind. The one thing I was grateful for was that before the accident happened, I could see things like flowers and colors before it was taken away from me. So, when someone described something, or I felt it, I could visualize it better than not having any background knowledge before.

As we continued down the path, I heard clanking noises to my right in the distance.

Once he finished describing the color of the roses we were passing, I quickly asked a question.

"What's that noise, Lord Jeren?" Even though I had a hunch what it was, I wanted to make sure.

"I beg your pardon, Your Highness?" He asked, confused.

"That noise, it sounds like swords clashing. Are we close to the training grounds?"

"Ah, yes, your highness, but don't worry, I won't take you any farther. We can go back, and I'll order some tea for you so that you can rest if you would like."

Then, a thought came to my mind. I knew the king trained hard, and maybe if he saw me out and about, he would not think me so frail.

"Actually, I would love to go to the training grounds."

"Oh, I assure you, there is nothing there worth…experiencing."

I appreciated his careful words, but I was no simpering princess.

"I would love to experience all of Maren. Even though I cannot see, I still like to experience all that you have to offer. That is if you don't mind."

"Not at all, Princess," he quickly responded, but I could hear some hesitation.

"Lead on, Lord Jeren."

The clashing of metal upon metal got louder with each step we took.

Then, a familiar voice that I was imprinted in my mind was shouting orders to his men.

King Rollan.

"Keep your eye on your opponent! That is a sure way to get yourself killed! ...Now, that's the spirit...use more force...Good job, men...Line up and try again."

I listened intently to every order, every command. My heart beat faster as he guided his men to give their best. This wasn't the cruel king my brother was worried about. He was a leader and someone *I* wanted to help lead me into the next phase of life. My stomach flipped as his deep voice entered my ears and pierced my heart.

I wish I knew what he looked like. While I have heard the rumors and didn't usually care, this one time, I wanted the same visual knowledge that brought the flowers to life that were so recently described to me.

"Your Majesty," Lord Jeren called out, and I froze. I had to force my hands to stay by their side and not reach up to touch my hair in the act of hoping I looked presentable. I prayed at least my gown would capture his attention if anything else failed.

Suddenly, a heavy silence filled the air. The sound of swords ceased immediately. I listened closely for the sound of footsteps that would indicate the King was walking towards us.

Either way, I put on a smile, hoping I didn't look dumb. Then, I imagined myself and decided to look neutral instead.

Sophia squeezed my arm to reassure me as the quiet moments passed, and I was grateful for her support as the silence continued. My heart picked up when I finally heard footsteps. I stood a little taller and waited for Lord Jeren to introduce His Majesty.

A few seconds passed, and I listened more carefully, only to hear the footsteps becoming softer and more distant.

"Oh…well… he must have not heard me," Lord Jeren's voice had a bitter edge to it, but I knew better.

My whole body flushed with embarrassment as the King disregarded me in front of all his men. What must they think of me?

I quickly shut down that train of thought before it ruined my day. I knew how easily it was to go down that dark hole of despair and how hard it was to get out.

Instead, I turned to Lord Jeren, plastered a smile on my face to hide my disappointment, and said, "that tea you offered earlier sounds delicious, Lord Jeren. After that lovely walk through the gardens, I think that would be just the thing to end this little tour."

"Oh, perfect. I'll have it sent right up to your room," his voice full of relief that I didn't understand what had just happened, at least in his eyes. I was glad to offer it. It wasn't his fault his King was acting rude.

"Thank you, and no need to escort us back," I patted my handmaiden's hand, "Sophia will take care of me."

After what had happened, I didn't know if I could handle being in anyone else's presence besides my handmaiden.

Sophia quickly escorted me back, and when we entered my room, I released my arm from her and went straight to the bed.

"I think I'll take a nap, Sophia."

"Yes, Princess," she said quietly, then after a moment, spoke again, her voice hesitant. "Are you sure you are alright? I know it's not my place, but…"

I turned in the direction of her voice and smiled, "I'll be just fine, Sophia. I appreciate your concern, but all I am is tired at the moment."

"Yes, Princess," her voice was small and full of doubt, but I didn't reassure her again.

I just wanted to crawl in bed and forget everything that had happened.

No one wanted me, not even the scarred king.

CHAPTER 6

ROLLAN

"How dare you embarrass the princess like that! In fact, I am embarrassed for you!"

I closed my eyes, waiting for my advisor to finish his lecture. My back was turned away from him as we stood in my study. I had avoided him for over three hours since the incident at the training grounds, but I knew I couldn't avoid him forever, and when I went back to my study after a while, he was there waiting for me.

"I had things to do besides entertain her. I was busy training my men." I turned slightly to my Commander, Davier, the one I ordered to continue the training while I escaped the training grounds, to see him looking at me with raised brows.

He was here for support while my advisor lectured me. Both men were my closest friends, which is why I sat through Jeren's lecture. You would think an advisor would be old, but Jeren was only a few years older than me, and his father was the advisor to mine. We also fought side by side in many battles. He was quick of mind, logical, and always thought two steps ahead, which was why I was baffled by his suggestion of marrying Princess Ellen.

"Don't make excuses to me! You not only embarrassed her but yourself. What kind of example are you setting for your men? You are a King; show some pride!"

"Pride!" I whipped around. "Is pride what got me this!" I pointed to my face.

He scowled, and we both knew I was acting childish. He lost a lot in the war as well. "I don't have time to escort a princess everywhere. I need someone who is efficient and can run the castle. This alliance was dead even before it started."

"You haven't even given it a chance!"

"I don't need to!" I hollered back.

Jeren closed his eyes and pinched his nose, collecting himself, and I waited, my temper rising.

"If you had taken time to get to know her, you would know that she does not need an escort. The only reason she had one today is because she is still learning the castle layout. She can efficiently run a castle and does so back at Kendall with the Queen's guidance, even if her brother doesn't recognize it. I would not suggest someone unworthy of you and running this kingdom. Do not let your pride get in the way of seeing what you only want to see because if you do…then who is *truly* the blind one?"

Then, without another word or dismissal, he turned around and left, leaving me speechless.

I turned to Davier, who had a look telling me that Jeren was right, even if he didn't say it out loud.

"Don't say anything," I pointed to him, and he held back a smirk.

After a moment, I stomped back into the hallway, grateful Jeren was not there. I turned right to make my way to my quarters since I was still sweaty from training and needed to calm down.

As I made my way down the hall, I started to hear soft music playing. It was a beautiful melody that seemed to pull at my hardened heart. Curiosity tugged me unconsciously towards the sound since music rarely filled the halls of my castle.

The closer I drew to the lovely music, the more I realized my temper started to fade, and the next thing I knew, I found myself standing right outside the door where the music was coming from.

I wondered who could possibly be playing. The only logical answer was the former Queen of Kendall. I was confused since I didn't recall seeing a harp with their luggage.

I leaned closer, the melody pulling at my very heartstrings. I needed to know who was playing this, but I didn't want to interrupt for fear they would stop.

"Excuse me, your majesty."

I quickly turned to see a maid standing beside me with a tea tray. My face heated from being caught listening outside the door. I stood tall, trying not to show my embarrassment.

She bowed, "I'm sorry, I just need to get inside."

Realizing I was still in her way, I stepped to the side and offered assistance.

"Here, let me get the door for you." Then I realized it was a blessing she was here. Now, I would get to see the mysterious harp player without lurking outside the door.

"Thank you for majesty." The maid bowed, and I opened the door, but it also gave me a chance to peek at who was playing.

I froze when I saw who it was and quickly started to back out of the room, but I was too slow.

The former Queen of Kendall had caught my eye and smiled brightly at me. She waved me inside the room and patted the seat next to her.

I tried to think of an excuse, but she raised her brows as if daring me to defy her. I took a big breath as if I was walking to my death and walked into the room full of beautiful music, where Princess Ellen was playing a song that sang straight to my heart.

I started to sit down in the chair across from the Queen, but she raised her brows once more and pointed with her head to the seat next to her.

I sat beside her, suddenly feeling uncomfortable, but right as my gaze hit her daughter's face, all I could think about was if angels ever lived on earth, they must look like her.

She wore a beautiful gold and cream-colored dress that matched her golden hair flowing down her back. Her skin was flawless. She closed her eyes as she concentrated on the music, her fingers plucking the strings and filling the air with a song that I never wanted to end.

How did I not notice her before?

I knew the answer right as I thought it. The same answer that made me so blind to her in the first place.

My advisor was right. I let my pride get in the way.

Now, as I sat here, listening to her play, a spell came over me.

"She plays beautifully, does she not," I turned to see the Queen so close to me that she could whisper without disturbing her daughter.

I nodded, "she does," I whispered back.

"She does more than just play. Don't let her blindness fool you, your highness. She is efficient in many things and doesn't let what happened to her stop her."

The Queen humbled me more than my advisor did.

I didn't respond, not knowing what to say. I had made such a fool of myself yesterday and today, but then the queen's words went through my mind again, and something caught my attention.

I turned back to the queen, knowing I was going to seem forward. "I hope this question isn't too prudent, but how did she become blind? You said she doesn't let what happened to her stop her. Was she not born blind?"

The queen smiled, "that is her story to tell."

I knew that all too well.

Suddenly, the music stopped, and we both turned to the Princess. I noticed her brow was pinched in worry, and I had the urge to wipe it away but quickly shook that thought. What was wrong with me? Didn't I want to stay away from her?

"Who are you talking to, mother? I thought I heard someone."

"No one, dear, just myself," the queen quickly announced before I could say anything.

I turned to her, and the queen winked at me, and I wondered what she was up to.

"Continue playing, darling. I know how it calms you down."

Embarrassment filled me. I knew exactly why she was upset since *I* was the reason. No doubt the queen knew as well. I couldn't look in her direction, so I continued to watch the princess, hoping and praying that by some miracle, I wasn't the reason she needed to calm down, but I knew it was.

She took a big breath, putting her hands down, only to raise them to wipe a tear from her cheeks.

"I can't, Mother. It's no use. The King hates me! Fredrick is right. We should have never come!"

My chest clenched, and I never regretted my actions so strongly before. I have always been prideful, but now I know I went too far. It didn't matter that women had run from me for years, and I made them feel frightened or uncomfortable. None of them ever cried for me, and if they did, it was because they couldn't wait to get away from me.

But her tears were not for that reason. In fact, it was the very opposite. She was sad because I wouldn't give her a chance.

"That's not true," Her mother soothed her. "We still have two days until the ball."

"No. He wouldn't even come and say hello in the gardens. I heard him walk away."

I couldn't breathe at her words and did not even dare to glance at the queen.

I'm such an oaf!

"He was probably busy, dear. I'm sure he didn't mean to."

Then I was surprised when I felt a gentle pat on my hand, and I looked at the Queen expecting a scolding, but a small smile is what I received.

I was confused. Why was she fighting for me after all I had done to her daughter?

No one, besides my advisor, commander, and men, ever fought for me.

"It doesn't matter. He'll never see me for anything other than blind. I've trained so hard with you for years, for what? So, Fredrick can keep me locked up in the castle."

"He loves you, dear, and is trying to protect you."

"Protection? More like imprisonment! I've proved to him over and over again that I can run a castle, but he is the one who turns a blind eye to me. Never seeing me for what I can do, but only for what I can't do. Just because I cannot see the world doesn't mean I am useless. I can listen. I can solve problems with the competence as much as the next man or woman."

"I know that, dear," the queen assured her.

"Yes, but no one else does. They think to treat me like a child, but I am grown. I want to love, to have a family one day just as much as anyone."

Love? I looked at this beautiful young woman and her confession. How could she think someone like me was capable of love?

"And you think the king can give you what you desire?"

I was shocked by the queen's question, but I suddenly had a burning desire to know the answer, so I didn't interject. What was wrong with me? Sitting here like some eavesdropper, waiting for the latest gossip. I know it was wrong. I should have gotten up and left the moment the princess started speaking, but I couldn't. I needed to know.

"I…I don't know," then she gave a look of defeat, and I hated her answer. I wanted to shout that I could love, but I didn't know if it was true. Love had not been a part of my life for a long time, not for eight years.

She continued. "Not after yesterday and today. I thought that maybe since we both had scars from our past, there would be something to connect from, to grow together with, but I was foolish. Not that I was expecting love, but…oh, Mother, what am I to do?"

More tears fell from her cheeks, and I clenched my fists to hold myself back from wiping them myself.

Suddenly, the princess stood up and bent to the ground beside her, picking up the long, skinny staff I had seen her use earlier.

She started to walk towards me, and I didn't know if I should jump up and leave before she did, but I didn't move.

I couldn't. I was frozen in my seat as I watched this beautiful girl, whom I've hurt, walk towards me. Guilt washed over me with how much my words and actions affected her. Of course, they would. Who would not be hurt by such rude declarations. I hated myself in that moment more than I had ever before. No amount of words behind my back, rejections over the years, could ever amount to how I felt at this moment. I truly felt like my heart was black and wondered if I could ever win back this princess's good graces.

I decided right then that's what I would do. I would prove to her that I wasn't the monster she and everyone thought me to be. Even if I wasn't capable of love, I could show some compassion.

Her walking staff bumped into my boot, bringing me out of my thoughts. She was so close, but I dared not move. Her brows pulled together as she tapped my boot with her walking staff.

"Fredrick?" she asked carefully, but I didn't correct her. "Mother, why didn't you tell me he was here?" when she flushed a deep red, I could no longer deceive her.

I stood up quickly and said the two words that barely ever left my mouth, but I meant them more than I had ever meant them before.

"I'm sorry."

Then I rushed out the door as if purgatory was chasing behind me.

CHAPTER 7

ELLEN

"Well, that was quite the confession," Mother spoke right after I heard the door shut, and I knew the King was no longer in our presence.

I wasn't usually a crier, but the tears seemed to flow. I was immediately wrapped up in my mother's loving arms.

"Oh, darling, I didn't think you would say anything on the matter, and he came in to hear your beautiful playing, and I knew if I told you he was here, you would have…well…maybe it's good he knows how you feel."

I felt like I was going to be sick. I knew she meant no harm; it was my own mouth that ran away with confessing my feelings when I thought it was just me and Mother. My head started to pulse, and I grew nauseous. I just confessed everything to the King. What must he think of me?

"Come sit down and drink something. You look like you are about to faint."

"I'm fine," I protested but sat down anyway, and more tears came. Not just because the King heard my words but because I knew that any chance I had of proving myself was gone. I didn't want pity from him, and even though he apologized, I couldn't help but feel it was out of obligation and that he didn't actually mean it.

"Here, darling," Mother told me and touched my hand, flipping it over before putting a teacup in it. "Drink this, then let us take a nap."

I sighed and drank deeply from the cup.

"I'm not tired," but I knew it was a lie. A headache was beginning to form, and I knew rest would do me good.

"Come now, let's not be stubborn, I already have your brother to deal with," she said in a playful tone.

I smiled, "and quite a handful he is."

"If you only knew."

Then we both laughed, and it felt good to relieve some of the stress from the moment.

After drinking some herbal tea, she led me back to my room. I was too drained from everything to even care about memorizing the castle layout or counting my steps.

Mother stopped, and I heard a door open.

"We are at your rooms, darling. I'll tuck you in and send a maid later to wake you."

"It's all right, Mother. I'm no child." Even though I felt childish after what had just happened.

"Hush, I'll not hear another word."

She led me inside, and I released my arm from her so I could walk to the bed with my walking staff since I memorized the layout already.

I turned around, "is there anyone here?" I didn't want to take any more chances before I spoke some more.

"No, just you and me. I'm sorry that I didn't tell you he was in the room."

"It's fine. I just…I don't think I'll go to the ball. There's no point after what happened."

"Are you sure?"

Yes? No? All I knew was that I didn't know where to go from here. I worked so hard to get here. To convince Fredrick to give me a shot, but I was naïve, and now I ruined it.

"Go to the ball," Mother encouraged me, "then we'll see how you feel. Who knows, you might change your mind."

I highly doubted it, but I would oblige her.

"Okay. But if I decided to leave…?" I left the question hanging.

"Then I'll take you straight home."

I smiled, "thank you, Mother."

"Now, get some rest. I'll check on you in a few hours."

It didn't take long for me to fall asleep. The only reprieve it seemed I would receive was the one in my dreams.

CHAPTER 8

ROLLAN

I headed straight back to my study, grateful that Jeren was no longer there. I didn't know if I could handle any more reprimands after the princess's confession.

I slumped in my seat behind my large wooden desk and looked over the papers that needed reviewing for my kingdom.

I couldn't concentrate and slammed the parchment back on the desk and sighed before running my fingers through my hair in frustration.

My fingers found my scar out of habit, and I ran my hand down the jagged edges, then back up again, feeling every bump and curve that reminded me of the sacrifices I have made for my kingdom. The sacrifices that Princess Ellen couldn't see. All she could see, or more like hear, was my words that made me the true monster in her mind. She didn't need to see me to know that I truly was broken.

"What have I done," I spoke out loud to myself. I needed to make things right with her, but I didn't know where to start. I stood up quickly. I needed to find Jeren. He would know what to do. I would take whatever tongue-lashing I deserved if it brought me back into the princess's good graces.

Right as I stepped around my desk to make my way to the door, a knock came from the outside.

Ah, good. Jeren was already here.

I sat back down before calling out. "Enter."

My eyes went wide with surprise when it wasn't my advisor who entered, but her Majesty, the Former Queen of Kendall.

I shot up and gave her a respectful bow, wondering what she must think of me after her daughter's confession.

"Come in, Your Majesty," I told her while motioning for her to sit in the chair across from my desk.

She settled down, and I was surprised she had a smile on her face, which confused me but didn't stop me from apologizing the second time today. A record, for sure.

"Your Majesty, I would like to apologize for what-"

She held up a hand to cut me off, and I immediately stopped speaking.

"Your majesty," she smiled. "It would seem there are a lot of misunderstandings going on, so I thought I would come to clear the air," she waved her hand in a circular motion, "if you will."

I nodded for her to continue.

"My daughter, though blind, has not used that as an excuse to sit idly and waste her life away. She works hard and, with my help, has not only learned to run a castle, but a kingdom. While her brother, as you know, does not see her in the same light I do and tries to protect her as any brother would, it is holding her back."

She took a big breath before continuing. "What I am about to tell you stays between us. While I was not expecting such a profound confession and just hoping for you to hear a beautiful talent she has worked hard at, such was not the case." Then she looked at me pointedly with raised brows. "My daughter did not come here out of pity or to mock you, as you have claimed."

Embarrassment flushed through me, and I cleared my throat since her words pierced my heart like an arrow, even though she spoke them with no malice.

"She came here because she saw something in you that others may not have seen. A man who has suffered much and is in need of a friend, just like she is in need of a friend. While she may not admit that, I know her better than anyone."

I scoffed, and she raised her brows with pinched lips in a look only a mother could give, daring me to defy her words. I felt like a child. Why couldn't I shove down my pride for one second? She was right, after all, even if I hated to admit it.

"I would also have you know that ever since she was young, she never looked upon appearances but how others treated their fellow man, and her blindness only seemed to enhance that profound characteristic many of us lack."

"So, what would you have me do? I have ruined any chance with her already."

"Firstly, do you even want her?" she asked boldly. "I will not waste my daughter's time when she will not be given the respect she deserves. She is not worthless and would make a fine queen to any Kingdom, given the chance."

I didn't have to sit there and contemplate my answer; my heart knew what it wanted, and if I could shove my pride down for a few seconds, I might actually make something of this strange arrangement.

"Yes," I confessed.

"Then what are you waiting for? Don't just be the King your kingdom needs, but the man your queen deserves. If it is my daughter, then prove it to her. I suggest letting her have the task of running the castle."

"Running the castle?" I wanted to add, *could she even do that? She is blind, after all*, but I held my tongue.

Then she stood up and walked to the door with her head held high. Right as she reached the door, she turned around to face me once more.

"Yes. I want you to know I am cheering for you, but there is only so much a former queen can do, even against her own son. I suggest you start making amends now."

Then she gave me another look, "and maybe as she proves to you that she is capable, you can prove to me that you are worthy of her."

Then she left without another word, leaving me feeling small, ashamed, and trying to think of ways I could make up for the fool I had been.

CHAPTER 9

ELLEN

I woke up to complete darkness. I was grateful that even though I lost most of my sight, I could still see some light, even though it was blurry.

"Sophia?" I called out to my maid, who always stayed close by. I was grateful for her diligence and commitment to me. I wouldn't know what I would do without her and Mother.

"Yes, Princess?" Her voice sounded as if I woke her up, and I felt bad.

"What time is it? How late did I sleep?"

Her voice was closer now, and I could hear her footsteps as she walked towards me. "The sun is just starting to rise. How are you feeling? Your mother came to check on you, and your headache had not subsided yet, so she sent for the healers. Did the medicine help?"

I laid back down, remembering yesterday's events and why I had a headache in the first place.

"Yes, it did help, but I don't think I'll be doing much today, anyway. I need you to start packing my trunks. We will be heading back after the ball, which I'm not sure I'll be attending."

"I'm sorry, Princess." I could hear the pity in her voice, but I didn't want pity. I wanted people to see me as a strong future ruler. Not the blind princess who couldn't do anything. I didn't want to stay here one more second if I wasn't wanted. I wasn't a dog who begged to his owner for some scrap of attention.

I heard the door push open and turned my head towards the sound, wondering who would barge in at this hour.

"Ah, good, you are awake," Mother's cheerful voice filled the room, and I let out a groan, which she ignored as she pulled back the drapes to let in more light.

"Sophia, grab the princess's blue gown with the gold ribbon."

What was she doing? I had to stop her before whatever plan she concocted got out of hand.

"Mother, what could possibly possess you to come here this early in the morning."

"We have a castle to run and a ball to prepare for and only a day to do it."

"What do you mean? I'm not even going to the ball," I asked, confused, "and it's not my job to run this castle, let alone prepare for a ball I will not even attend."

"Nonsense. As a future queen of this kingdom, we need to put our best foot forward and take the reins. Prove to them that I've trained you well in running a castle and kingdom."

"Mother, I'm sure everything is already taken care of. I don't think King Rollan wants us barging in. He already doesn't like the fact that-"

Another knock on the door interrupted me.

"Just in time," Mother chirped, and I heard her footsteps approaching the door. I prayed it wasn't the King. I didn't know if I could be in his presence so soon after what had happened yesterday. Not to mention, I just woke up, and was probably a sight to see.

"Come in, Lord Jeren."

Lord Jeren? King Rollan's advisor? What was he doing here so early in the morning?

"I apologize, but the princess seems to be having a late start this morning. She wasn't feeling well yesterday, as you know. Could we meet in the main foyer in about twenty minutes?" Mother asked him.

"Yes, that sounds wonderful, Your Majesty. I look forward to working with Princess Ellen from here on out."

The door shut, and I was pulled out of bed with Sophia's hand working quickly to get me dressed and do my hair for the day.

I finally broke the silence after I had a moment to breathe.

"Mother, I don't think this is a good idea."

"I will not hear another word about it. Lord Jeren thinks it's an excellent idea."

"While his advisor may think so, what about his Majesty?"

"I think you'll find he may be more agreeable than we might have previously thought."

I highly doubted that but didn't say it out loud.

I heard her step in front of me; then, she gently grabbed my shoulders.

"Today, I want you to put everything I have taught you into practice. Do it with the confidence that any future queen would be proud of." Then she spoke softly. "Can you do that for me, Ellen?"

I took a big breath, not wanting to agree, but I would humor her. All I had to do was get through the next few days.

"Yes."

Then her hand went to my cheek, cupping it with motherly love, "and you will do wonderful."

I prayed she was right.

"Now," she quipped, "let's go."

Soon, I was shoved out the door and led to the foyer where Lord Jeren was supposed to meet us. I wondered if he would bring up what happened yesterday at the training grounds, and I was grateful when he didn't.

"Princess, you look absolutely stunning," he said with a cheerful voice.

"Thank you," I had to force my hands to stay where they were instead of raising them to my hair and touching it out of self-consciousness, even though I knew Sophia did excellent work and never let me leave the room unless I was perfect.

"Today, I was hoping you would help me with the last of the preparations for the ball tomorrow."

I put my shoulders back and raised my head high with the confidence Mother had taught me. "It would be my honor to help you."

"Perfect. Well, let us get started, shall we," he clapped his hands together, then introduced me to the head housekeeper, Mrs. Warson. She read off the list of preparations that had already been accomplished and what we would work on today and tomorrow morning.

A feeling of excitement overcame me, which was so different from a few minutes ago when I previously wanted to hop in the carriage and leave. I didn't realize how desperate I was to prove myself, and now that the opportunity arose, I wanted to dive in with full force.

I was also surprised by how smoothly I took over the role of making sure things were done in order and rearranging some assignments to ease the burden of the servants. They were splitting too many of the larger chores when it would be faster if they combined their efforts on some things while splitting others. I made sure to thank them for their work to let them know they were appreciated and needed. Even if it wasn't my castle, I was now helping prepare and wanted them to know that their efforts did not go unnoticed.

"I think we are going to get along quite nicely, princess. It's nice to have a woman's touch in these halls." Mrs. Warson spoke with a voice that made me feel like she meant it, and I almost regretted leaving so soon. It felt good to take control, especially when my brother was constantly hovering over me, which made me wonder where he was at the moment, but I wouldn't dare ask for fear that he may pop up and fate would have its final laugh.

"I also wanted to inform you that the walls have been cleaned, and I have assigned maids to keep up with the task."

I blushed from embarrassment but was grateful. Even though I wouldn't be here long, it would be nice to be able to guide myself around the castle without my fingers turning black from the dust.

"Thank you, Mrs. Warson. I'm hoping it won't be needed for long, but I appreciate your efforts."

We then made our way to the kitchen to confirm the menu, and I was able to sample dishes that were native to these lands. Everything was delicious, and I couldn't wait to taste the entire meal.

"May I ask what the options are for dessert?" I asked Chef Brandly.

"Oh, you're in for a treat, princess. We have our fresh berry tarts, made with a special sauce," then I felt his presence as he came close and whispered, "A plum sauce." I smiled at his whispered secret before tasting the delicate treat.

"It's absolutely divine." And it truly was.

"Thank you, your highness. We are pleased to serve you and hope you find all of our dishes to your liking."

"I'm sure I will." Then, a thought popped into my head. "And what is His Majesty's favorite dessert?"

"Ummm…" came the hesitant voice of the head cook, and I wondered if the King didn't like dessert.

"Candied nuts," came a deep voice from across the room near the door we had entered earlier, and I froze.

The whole room went quiet, followed by a chorus of "Your Majesty."

I turned towards the man with whom I had hoped not to run into today, which was a ridiculous thought since it was his castle, after all.

"Your Majesty," I spoke and curtsied, wanting to be anywhere but here. What must he think about me taking charge? Did his advisor ask him before setting me on this task?

I heard his footsteps, heavy boots coming towards me.

"But what is the princess's favorite dessert? After all, the ball is hosted in her honor?"

Was he mocking me or actually curious? I couldn't tell, but I straightened to my full height before answering.

"Cake with fresh strawberries and whipped cream on top, but after tasting the delicious berry tarts, I might have to change that."

The room was silent after my reply. I couldn't even hear the stirring of a pot as I waited for the King to respond.

"An excellent choice, no doubt," then his footsteps told me he left, along with the relief of breaths that filled the room.

CHAPTER 10

ROLLAN

I watched from the shadows and saw the moment she came down the stairs to the foyer like some lovesick fool hiding away, but I was no lovesick fool, just a curious one. I couldn't deny how beautiful she looked and was grateful she no longer looked sick and pale from yesterday's events. My gut clenched with how I treated her.

Yesterday, after the queen left, I called Jeren to my study to tell him my plan. He agreed readily, and while the princess was resting, my advisor and I made plans to make amends to the Princess. I had him relay the message to the former queen, who was eager to join in.

Watching her from the shadows, I realized how wrong I had been about the Princess. She took matters into her own hands with a grace and beauty that these castle walls had not seen for a long time. Not ever since my mother died. I noticed people were at ease around her and tried to please her, for which I was grateful. I wanted them to respect and do her every wish, not to take advantage because of her blindness.

It also made me jealous. While I demanded order and perfect obedience, it also made those under my command fear me. I often wondered if they followed my orders for fear of the retribution I would give if they did not obey. Not Ellen, though. They looked eager to please her. I've never seen my housekeeper smile so much or more eager to please than I have at this moment. I followed them as they made their way to the kitchen. Jeren, who was ever observant, saw me and raised his brows to see if he should announce me, but the slight shake of my head told him not to.

A stayed far enough behind until the cook's attention was thoroughly engrossed by the princess. Then, when she asked what my favorite dessert was, I had to make myself known. I don't know why, but some part of me wanted her to know. It was ridiculous and really didn't matter, but at that moment, I wanted to be the one to tell her.

The room went quiet as everyone turned to me and gave their respects. The room grew heavy with tension, and I hated that I was the one who broke the spell the princess had over them, but I had to know her answer, and I wondered why she even cared about mine.

To be honest, I did not have a sweet pallet. Savory was more my preference when it came to food, but candied nuts around the holidays were always my favorite.

When she responded with her answer, I wanted to change the menu to please her, but instead complimented her on her choice and left quickly, feeling as if my presence was not wanted, which was probably true. I was never wanted, except as a voice to run my kingdom. No one wanted me…except for her.

Why, though?

I remembered the conversation she had with her mother that my ears were not supposed to hear, then later with the Queen herself.

Did she truly not come here out of pity? Was friendship what she desired?

I growled out loud and saw my knights straighten as I walked by, but I didn't care. My thoughts turned over the last few days and how I acted towards her. Would she want to be my friend now with how I treated her? Was she now staying to fulfill the obligation between our kingdoms, and then once the time period was over, would she leave?

I didn't think so. Her brother would not allow it. He was as stubborn as me.

Did the queen force her to stay for the month, or was she willingly trying to show me that she could be the kind of queen my kingdom needed?

Did I even want a friend? I've heard of many arranged marriages that were based on mutual respect with no love or friendship between them. Is that what I wanted? Experience told me, yes. Friendship only brought pain in the end. My older brother was my best friend. We fought side by side in the war, and losing both him and my father to our enemy brought an unbearable pain that felt like death itself.

These dark thoughts swirled in my mind as I made my way out of the castle doors and to the training grounds. My temper tainting my soul, and only the thought of training with my men could release the anger building up inside me—my only solace from the pain of losing everything and everyone I had loved.

It was a good thing I didn't stay and escort the princess on her duties around the castle, even though that was what I yearned to do. My darkened spirit would have put a damper on her and everyone else's day as I questioned her and her mother's motives. My mere presence killed the sunshine she brought to the castle.

I walked to the armory and picked up a practice sword, then made my way out to the training grounds and was surprised when I saw my men training with King Fredricks guards.

I watched from a distance, my thoughts turning to the day they came. Maybe he was right; I didn't deserve his sister. I didn't deserve the happiness she brought. She couldn't even see the light she brought into the room. She was so innocent, lovely, and beautiful, inside and out.

And I was a monster.

I scowled and made my way into the rink with those training. My men immediately stopped training and faced me, giving me slight bows.

It was right then King Fredrick noticed me, and he put up a hand for his opponent to stop and turned towards me.

"Come to train?" He asked me with a mocking voice. I didn't say anything; I just glared. I could easily defeat him, but I wasn't one to boast. Only weak men bolstered themselves up. I knew my strength and didn't need to prove it to anyone.

I looked toward my commander and gave him a nod to continue training.

"I know," Fredrick walked up to me with a smirk on his face, "how about a little wager?"

All the men stopped and looked towards us at his words.

"I don't bet, your majesty."

He scoffed out loud, then glared back at me. "Then a friendly match perhaps?"

I crossed my arms, not saying anything. He obviously wasn't going to let this drop.

He stepped up to me, sizing me up, and my men shifted towards me, but I held up a hand for them to stop.

"What do you want?" I asked with as much indifference as I could muster, trying my best to keep the annoyance out of my voice.

He leaned close so that no one else would hear.

"My sister."

I glared. What was he saying?

"For some reason, she wants to stay in this forsaken place, but if I had my way, I would take her away this instant."

My blood boiled at his words while a strange ache entered my heart as I imagined her leaving the castle. I shoved those foreign emotions down. It would happen either way. I might as well face the reality of it.

"Then do it," I threatened. I was tired of his game. It was better that she left sooner than later, with how quickly I was becoming attached.

No, I wasn't attached. I was just curious, that was all. Did I even need this alliance with them anyway? I didn't want war, but it seemed he would start one over his sister if I stepped one toe out of line.

He pulled back, his arms out to the side, "I can't," he stated. "And it isn't just my sister, but my mother who is against it, but that's where this little...*endeavor* comes in."

I could tell he was refraining from using wager, but I knew better.

"Spit it out, man, I don't have all day. While your men may be lacking, mine are not, and you are cutting into our training time."

His face turned red at my words, and I held back a smile at how I caused him to react.

"Fine. If I win, you break off the alliance, and I get to take my sister back to Kendall."

"Just take her now if you are so eager."

He laughed, "It's not so simple. I will be made the villain in her eyes, even if I told her it was for her own good. Which I have, mind you. I need you to break it, and you must tell her yourself and the queen."

"I almost wonder who rules your Kingdom?" I chided.

His face went beet red. I almost enjoyed getting under his skin.

"At least I have the heart to do what is right. I care about those around me and would do anything to protect them. That's what a *true* King does."

He knew nothing of protecting his kingdom, but I kept the words to myself. I wouldn't explain myself to him. A King never did.

"And if I win?" I asked.

"It will be a waiting game. We will stay the whole three months, but I know what she'll choose in the end. It's obvious, is it not," he smirked, and I had the urge to punch him right in the jaw.

I took a deep breath, knowing I would show him soon enough just what he got himself into. I almost regretted picking up a practice sword since the blade was dull. I wished I would have brought my real sword to this match.

I held out my hand for him to take, and he grasped it firmly.

He smiled as if he had already won, but little did he know.

"Davier!" I called out to my commander while still looking at Fredrick. "Have all the men stand outside the rink. His majesty is about to lose a bet."

Fredrick smiled, not even taunted by my words, and ordered his men to do the same.

I shrugged off my leather jacket, leaving me in my white shirt and training pants. I wanted nothing restrictive, even though it provided more protection.

Davier approached me and took the jacket from my hands, "what are you doing, your majesty?" he whispered.

"Just a friendly wager," I told him, but his raised brows told me that he knew it was a lie. I was ruthless, and my men knew it, and the King of Kendall was about to know it, too.

He didn't say anything else as he went to the fence and climbed over to be with our men.

I looked back and saw his majesty waiting for me in the middle of the grounds, and I couldn't wait to wipe that smirk off his face.

I met him in the middle, and we raised our swords up in front of us as protocol called for.

"May the best King win," I told him.

He chuckled. "Don't worry, I will."

I turned and walked three steps away before facing him, not giving into his jibe.

"Ready?" Davier called out to us, and I gave him a nod.

"The best two out of three! Let's begin!" he yelled, and we started to circle each other. Our focus now on the game before us. One I was determined not to lose.

He made the first move by lunging at me, and I blocked it easily.

We parried back and forth, getting a feel for one another. Minutes went by as our swords clashed in the dance of warriors, neither of us getting any closer to striking the other down.

The sun was soon high in the sky, and sweat started to drip down our faces and soak our shirts. As we circled, I noticed the light catch his eye, and in a split second, when he blinked the light away, I brought my sword up and around quickly to touch his arm just below his shoulder when his defenses dropped.

If we were using real swords, it would have cut right through, but he would only have a bruise tomorrow due to my control.

"One to zero," Davier called out, and Fredrick growled. This time, *I* couldn't keep the smirk off my face.

He started to move quickly, and once our circling stopped, we lunged back and forth, taking turns striking each other and trying to find a hole in each other's defenses.

I stepped back so we could take a break from our challenge, but my heel caught on something and made me lose my balance for half a second. I quickly righted myself just in time to block Fredrick's strike, but he quickly brought his sword around to strike his first blow on my thigh.

Pain seared up and down my leg, as he stepped back with a wide grin.

I took a big breath, blocking out the pain as I shook out my leg.

"Fredrick, what in the name of all that is good are you doing!?"

We both turned to see the Queen standing outside the training grounds, watching us with a shocked expression and deep disapproval.

But that's not what caught my eye. The princess was making her way over with my advisor. She hung onto his arm. They must have been heading toward the gardens, but the ruckus of Fredrick's and mine guards cheering for us must have brought them over to see what was happening.

"Nothing, Mother. Just a friendly little competition," her son called back to her, his look daring me to defy his words and disclose our little wager.

I wasn't so dishonorable.

"Well, stop it this instant! You could get yourself killed. Do you know who this King is?"

It was true. I fought my way through hundreds of men to save our kingdom, and I paid dearly for it.

"I know *exactly* who he is," he called back, his gaze never leaving mine, but I had a feeling his words didn't mean what he wanted his mother to think.

"We're almost done, Mother. Go to the gardens, and I'll meet you there," he dismissed her, and I watched her reaction.

She held her head high but turned to take her daughter's arm from Jeren and whisper something in her ear.

The princess's eyebrows raise. The queen must have told her what was going on. I wondered what Ellenora would think of our little wager. Would she want to stay?

I would give it a chance it deserved, and my determination grew as I looked over the beautiful princess before me, grateful she could not see my gaze, not caring that others did. They would know I did this for her, even if she didn't.

I faced her brother, "let's finish this," I snarled, then I lunged at him with all my might, my blows twice as strong as before. I was holding back, but not anymore.

I brought up my sword, and Fredrick went to block it, but I quickly pivoted and brought it back down for the final and winning blow, making him stumble back and hold his arm where I had hit.

My men's cheers filled the training grounds as they raced out to congratulate me.

I smiled as they hoisted me onto their shoulders, claiming me the winner.

"It's not over," Fredrick called out over my men, and I turned to see him smiling as if he hadn't just lost. "She could still refuse you."

Then he walked away as the truth hit me.

I might have one this round, but it only gave me time. I looked over at the beautiful girl I still had to win over and only three months to prove how sorry I was for how I acted towards her when she first came. Then, if she did accept my apology, I had to prove that I was a man worth loving, even if others did not think so, and that I could love her in return if she would only give me a chance.

That I wasn't the monster that everyone thought me to be.

As my men carried me back to the castle, I watched as her brother made his way over to her. Would he tell her what happened? Would she regret that I won? I didn't feel like the winner they thought me to be as scenes of first meeting her flashed across my mind, and I knew I would regret them until the day I died.

CHAPTER 11

ELLEN

An ear splitting cheer erupted into the air, and my heart raced with anticipation.

I clung to Mother tightly. "Who won?" I asked eagerly, wishing I still had my eyesight.

"The king," she stated teasingly.

"Which one?" desperation in my voice.

"King Rollan."

My heart soared. I didn't know what little game my brother was playing, but I'm glad he lost since I knew it had something to do with me, not that I would tell him, because once I heard his voice coming near, I put on a sorrowful expression.

"What happened?" I asked him innocently after he greeted us.

"Nothing, just a little training with the king. The men wanted to see us spar, so we humored them."

I knew he was lying, but I didn't press for more answers.

"Which was a foolish thing to do," Mother scolded him. "You have better things to do than cause mischief when we are trying to build an alliance."

"It might not even happen," he snapped back. "Ellen still has a choice."

"And if I choose to stay?" I called out. I was tired of them talking about me as if I was some cripple who couldn't make decisions. Just because I lost my eyesight didn't mean I wasn't sound of mind. Well, my mother knew that, but Fredrick continued to treat me like I was glass, ready to break at any moment.

"It's my life, Fredrick, and I will choose what is best for me."

I was surprised when he didn't argue back, and even though we were surrounded by noise, the tension between us drowned everyone out.

"I'm going to change," was all he said, and I heard his footsteps fade.

"Is he gone?" I whispered to Mother after a few moments.

"Yes, but I'm afraid that's not the end of it. He is stubborn, especially when it comes to you." Then she spoke softly, just for my ears only, "Don't be too harsh on him. He loves you and cares for you deeply. He'll forever regret that day."

I immediately felt bad for snapping back at him. I knew he cared and loved me deeply, but he needed to let the past go. I forgave him for what happened, but he seemed to punish himself no matter what I said.

"I know, it's just hard," I told her.

She squeezed my hand to reassure me.

I waited a few moments before asking a question burning on my tongue. I didn't want to seem too eager. "Is King Rollan still here? I wanted to congratulate him on his win."

"His men carried him inside on their shoulders as the victor."

"Oh," I said, letting my disappointment seep through. I would have to make sure the next time I saw him, I would congratulate him, and maybe he would tell me more about the friendly little competition they had.

"I think it's time for a break. Maybe some lemonade?" Mother asked me.

"Sounds divine."

We spoke with Lord Jeren to meet up in a couple of hours to continue our preparations for the ball, then made our way up to my room where Mother called for lemonade and some refreshments, but my thoughts were back at the training grounds and wondering what my brother and the King were fighting over.

"You aren't drinking very much," Mother asked softly, interrupting my thoughts, "what seems to be the matter?"

I took a sip before setting my teacup down on the table and decided to tell her my thoughts.

"What do you really think was happening out there at the training grounds?"

"No doubt, it was about you," she told me with quick confidence.

My cheeks burned at her words, but then my thoughts took over, and worry settled instead, "do you think it was to break the alliance?"

"I'm not sure, but I'll know soon enough."

"I don't know. It seemed Fredrick was keen on keeping the reason to himself."

"He may be King, Ellen, but I am still his Mother."

We both chucked at that statement. Mother was loving and kind, but she also had a way of getting information when she wanted it.

"Now, I think we should rest before we finish the preparations for the ball and get ready to have dinner with the King."

Every meal we've had so far, even though we've only been here a few days, and one of those I wasn't feeling well, his presence was absent.

"He probably won't be there," I told her, but it was more for me, so I wouldn't get my hopes up.

"You may be surprised. Now, why don't you rest while I go search for your brother and do some digging."

I smiled, then called for my handmaiden to assist me to bed.

I heard Mother get up and make her way toward the door, opening it up slowly. When her footsteps didn't enter into the hallway and fade away, I turned towards her.

"Is everything all right, Mother?" Wondering if someone was outside the door or coming towards us in the hallway.

"I just wanted to say how brave you are, darling. Many would hide away, but not you. You push forward and bring a light to those around you. Don't ever let that light diminish. You keep on shining, darling."

Then I heard the door close as tears filled my eyes because I was grateful I had a mother who always knew what I needed to hear.

My nerves shook as Mother led us to the main dining area where we would have dinner with King Rollan. I wouldn't worry about memorizing the castle layout now. Who knew if I would even need to? The past few days since I've been here, any interaction we've had so far has not been ideal, but I was hoping tonight might change that. The ball was tomorrow, and I was either leaving or staying, and tonight, depending on how the conversation went, would tell me which one was in my future.

A sad feeling swept over me. I didn't want to leave, but I also would not stay where I was not wanted, but the thought of going home so soon made me feel like a failure.

"Chin up, darling," Mother told me softly, and I realized she could see my countenance. "We are almost to the doors and shortly will be in the presence of King Rollan."

I put my shoulders back and took a big breath as I heard the door open. Even if he were not there, I would enter with the grace and confidence worthy of my status.

"Smile, Ellen, the night is still young," my mother encouraged me.

I put on a small smile. I didn't want to look silly walking into the room with a full grin on my face and have the King think me mad. He already thought I was a joke.

I heard the scraping of chairs.

"I'm glad you made it," My brother's voice filled the air, but right after, another voice spoke that made my heart stop.

"Your Majesty. Princess."

I could hear footsteps coming our way. I tried to swallow, but it caught in my throat as I wondered who was approaching us. My brother or…

I held my breath in anticipation.

"My sister. As beautiful as always," Fredrick spoke louder than usual with a reprimanding tone that was no doubt aimed to rebuke the King and let him know what a fool he was.

"Fredrick," I hissed through my teeth quietly, letting him know to quit this behavior.

"What?" he told me innocently," can a brother not compliment his sister?

I sighed. "Yes, thank you." Then, I steered the conversation away from me. "I'm glad you came. We've missed you at almost every meal since we've been here."

He usually took his meals in his rooms, but I knew why he was here tonight.

"And leave you in the hands of this man?" he scoffed, "hardly."

"Quiet, he might hear you," I told him after having enough of his behavior.

"Good."

My annoyance flared, but I held it in. He was going to ruin everything if he kept running that mouth of his, but I didn't want to make a scene, so I held my tongue.

"I was hoping the Princess might sit next to me," King Rollan called out as my brother led me to the table, grateful he didn't make any more sneering remarks.

My brother stiffened, but my heart fluttered. Maybe there was still hope? Even if he did hear my brother, he was not letting his rudeness affect us.

I knew I shouldn't be reacting this way, not after his insults to me, but I couldn't help but think about his apology today.

Did he truly mean it? He was here now, wasn't he, and that had to mean something.

My brother tugged me closer to him, shaking me from my thoughts, and before he told the King, *"no,"* I responded.

"I would be honored," I turned toward the King's voice and tugged my brother to lead me the way, but I didn't have to go far since my hand was soon grabbed by one that was larger and calloused, sending flutters to my stomach and heat to my cheeks. I heard my brother sigh and step away as the King led me around the room. We stopped, and he released his soft grip on my hand to pull out the chair for me.

"Please, sit," King Rolan told me and gently grabbed my hand again to guide me to my chair. His touch sending sparks up my arm.

I sat as he pushed the chair under my knees. I tried my best to settle myself as he took his seat next to me, but instead, I held my breath in anticipation. I never thought this would happen while I was here. Maybe miracles were a real thing. They had to be after today.

"Let us eat," the King called out, and I could feel the presence of someone lean over and put a plate in front of me. A delicious aroma filled my nose, and I could tell it was some sort of poultry dish. Meanwhile, the dining room filled with the voices of those attending the meal.

"It smells delicious," I told the King while putting my fingers on the edge of the table to feel for the utensils.

"Thank you. We have an excellent cook."

"I agree. Meeting him today was a treat, literally."

He chuckled at my reference of trying the berry tarts, and I couldn't help the smile that came to my face. I barely recognized the man sitting next to me.

Then he fell silent for a moment, and I took the opportunity to slowly put my fork down until I hit some food on the plate, making sure to get a small size to eat.

"Your brother is right. You look stunning, Princess," he whispered close to my ear, his breath on my skin, which didn't help settle my reaction to him. In fact, it only made it worse.

"Thank you," I spoke softly while setting my fork down, hoping my voice didn't betray how he was making me feel.

"I'm sorry for how I behaved the last few days. Seeing you today has made me realize what a fool I have been, and…" he paused, taking a big breath, "would you please allow me to have a second chance? To prove I am not the monster that rumors have played me out to be, even though I acted as such."

He wanted redemption. At first, I thought I was so sure and willing to give it to him, but now that he asked, I wondered if this was the right course. But as quickly as those thoughts came, they left, and I knew my answer.

"Of course, but…"

I paused, and I could hear his feet shift.

"Yes?"

His voice was so near, and I could barely think, but I knew I needed to speak my peace.

"As I give you a second chance, I also ask for one for myself. See me as a person, not just as a girl who is blind. I am more than my eyesight, your Majesty."

"Rollan."

I smiled at his permission to use his given name, even though that is what I have been calling him all along in my mind.

"Of course. In fact, it's probably best that you...well..."

He was being very hesitant, and I didn't want him to be. If this was going to work between us, I wanted him to trust me fully with everything.

"Yes?" I prompted him to continue.

"I'm afraid that along with internal scars, I also have visible ones."

He was worried that if I had my eyesight, I would judge him before getting to know him.

"I meant what I said the first day I was here," as desperate as I was to try and forget it. "I don't, and now can't," I laughed to make light of my situation, "judge people by their looks. I base it on their heart."

"Well, I hope to redeem mine," his voice was full of hope.

I smiled, "well, if you have those berry tarts for dessert I tried earlier today, then you have nothing to worry about."

He chuckled, and my heart soared at the deep and alluring sound that filled my ears. I wanted to make him laugh again just so I could hear it.

"You can have them whenever you desire, Princess. As long as you stay."

Stay? He wanted me to stay?

"I would like nothing more."

CHAPTER 12

ROLLAN

She was beautiful in every sense of the word. When she came into the dining room, my breath was stolen from my chest. I was so mesmerized by her presence that her brother got to her before I could even step away from the table, but I wouldn't let that deter me.

When King Fredrick entered the room, we sat in silence until my advisor came to break the contention building between us, which is why I couldn't let him take her away from me. It also provided a private moment to ask her for forgiveness, even though I knew I didn't deserve it. Yet, she proved me wrong once again with how truly forgiving and beautiful her soul was, and it called to me even stronger than the call of duty to my kingdom.

I realized I would do anything to become in her good graces once more.

I watched as the food was set before her. She spoke a soft thank you, lifted her hand up to feel for the utensils, and slowly started to cut the food. While she was proficient, a burning need to help her coursed through me.

"Let me cut your food for you," I offered.

She put her utensils down and turned to me.

"I'm not so helpless as all that, your Majesty," she teased.

"I know, I just thought…" embarrassment filled me, and I felt like a fool. I probably made her feel inadequate when I just wanted to help.

She reached over until her hand found my arm, "thank you for being so thoughtful," she assured me, then went back to cutting her food.

"It smells divine," She breathed in the food deeply, "may I ask what it is."

"Buttered potatoes with gravy, candied carrots, chicken, and a roll."

"No berry tarts?" Her voice sounded disappointed, but her smile told me she was joking.

"Not yet," I smiled at her teasing, and it did something glorious to me.

"Well, then I guess it will have to do, your Majesty," she faked a sigh.

I laughed, and it felt so good. The only thing that would make me feel better was if she called me Rollan again, but now that we were among company, I knew she wouldn't.

I felt someone watching us, and I turned to look down at the table and saw my advisor staring at me with wide eyes. I guess his reaction was justified; I didn't remember the last time I had laughed. My life had too much pain and sorrow to bring that emotion to my life.

Then he smiled widely and returned to speaking with the Queen and King Fredrick. I was grateful he kept their attention for now so I could have the princess all to myself without her brother butting in.

I returned my attention to the princess and watched as she slowly brought her fingers back to the edge of the table to set her knife down, then skimmed along the edge until she found the spoon. I tried not to stare as she slowly put her spoon down, scooped up some potatoes, and ate them carefully and delicately. I tried to focus on my own meal but was finding it hard to do. She was the very meaning of perfection. If the word had a face to it, it would be hers.

"Do I have something on my face, your Majesty?" she slightly turned to me, and my face heated with embarrassment, realizing that even though she was blind, she could probably sense my stare.

"No," I coughed out, embarrassed at being caught and dug into my meal quickly to cover my blunder.

"So, tell me about Maren. If the alliance…" she paused, then said, "I would love to hear about your kingdom."

My heart pounded…*if the alliance what? Worked?* I wanted to ask, but didn't have a chance.

"Yes, do tell us all about Maren, your Majesty," came her brother's voice from down the table. I didn't miss the snarky way he said it.

I quickly looked up at him to see him watching me with eyes that were sending daggers straight at my chest. I gave him my own look, telling him I didn't miss the tone he spoke with.

I quickly ignored him, turned back to his sister, and asked, "What would you like to hear?"

I side glanced at her brother and saw his focus didn't leave us. I wanted to give him a cold remark, maybe remind him he lost the little bet *he* suggested in the training grounds, but that wouldn't make me win his sister's hand any faster, and I wasn't about to lose Ellen over my pride.

"What is your main stock or goods that you trade with?"

I paused, taken back by her question. I thought she would ask me about the latest fashion trend or the gossip of the court, but deep down, I knew that wasn't the kind of person she was.

"Well, we have several mines that produce several different metals-"

"Which I have heard you've been asking double in price for," Fredrick interrupted.

"Fredrick, would you mind yourself!" Ellen scolded him.

He pushed back his chair and made his way over toward us, and I wanted to tell him his company wasn't wanted, but I held my tongue. I also noticed the room got quiet, and everyone's attention was now on us, but I ignored it in hopes they would go back to their conversations when they realized nothing was wrong.

Fredrick sat down and stared at me pointedly. Maybe this wouldn't work, and I was trying to win her hand for nothing.

"I'm just here for some friendly political talk, Ellen. After all, we might be allies shortly, and you know what they say…"

"What do they say," I asked with raised brows.

He leaned close to me, "keep your friends close…" he raised his brows, then leaned back and smiled, making his meaning clear. I knew the unfinished phrase he was making a point with, but the only enemy he was making here was that of himself.

"As I was saying," *before I was rudely interrupted,* I added only to myself. Then I proceeded to tell the Princess all about the mines and the men that worked them. "The reason we sell it at a higher price than before is because my men and women put their lives at risk every day when they go into the mines," then I turned to Fredrick. "And isn't a man's life worth more than meager pay? Don't they have families to feed, clothe, and shelter like we do? Surely, you treat your own people the same way?"

He pinched his lips, and I smiled smugly at him when he didn't respond.

"I think that is fair, and I'm sure your people work harder because of the generosity you give them," Ellen smiled at me.

"I try to be fair in every way I can, even though I often fall short." I thought of the main one; how every woman refused to be my wife, except for her. Then I stopped and looked at Ellen and wondered if she could see, what would she think of me? Would she run away like every other courtier I've met, or would she really look past my scars that were more than surface deep and truly love me, or at least agree to the marriage alliance? I knew our marriage would not be based on love, but as I looked at the curve of her face and straight, small nose that seemed perfect in every way, my heart yearned for that. It wasn't just her beauty or pity, as some might claim. It was something deeper. Her determination and confidence seemed to shine from within.

She smiled. "Don't think so little of yourself. Even though my brother is stubborn, he wouldn't be here, and neither would I if he didn't think you ran your kingdom fairly and justly."

Her brother grunted, and he folded his arms and turned away, neither denying nor accepting her words. I wondered if what she said was true. If he really thought that I was some horrid king, would he have not even considered bringing his sister? The evidence was before me, and it gave me hope.

We talked until it grew late, telling each other about our lives and growing up. The only question I didn't ask was how she lost her eyesight. I was afraid to offend or embarrass her when the night was going so well, not that I was eager to talk about my own scars. It wasn't until the Queen was heading to bed that I realized how fast the time had gone.

"Come, darling, we must get you well-rested for tomorrow's ball."

She stood up, and I did as well. "Until tomorrow, Princess."

She curtsied, "Thank you, your majesty. I look forward to it."

As I watched them leave, I anticipated the ball with enthusiasm. For the first time, I was excited to host such a significant event because that meant a beautiful princess, who had somehow squeezed into my heart, would be dancing in my arms for most of the evening, and not even her brother could stop that.

CHAPTER 13

ELLEN

"There," my mother gently patted my shoulders right as my handmaiden finished my hair. "You look absolutely beautiful,"

I took a deep breath in.

"What's wrong, darling? Are you having second thoughts?"

"No," I quietly assured her, but I knew it wasn't true.

"I made your brother promise to be on his best behavior tonight."

I waved her comment away, "It's not that. I...I just..."

I didn't know how to explain it to her. I was so confident when it came to running the castle, but now that I thought about all the people of the court who would be at the ball and the comments I would receive, doubt started to rush in.

Mother gently turned me towards her. Even though I couldn't see her, I knew I was about to receive some wisdom.

"Why did you come here?"

I was taken aback by her question when I thought she would build up my confidence.

"To help form an alliance with our kingdoms?"

"No. Why did *you* come here?"

I didn't answer right away since I didn't know if I knew the answer myself. I was sure of my reasons earlier, but now?

I felt lightheaded, and my stomach twisted with anxiousness.

"Did you come here out of pity for the King?"

"No!"

"No?"

Then everything I was feeling spilled out of my mouth.

"I know it might seem that way. That I am the only kind of person who could marry him because I'm blind, or that he's desperate for an heir, or that my kingdom is so desperate for an alliance they'll give their crippled daughter away, but it is so much more than that! Not only do I want to live my life to the fullest, but I feel this connection that...that I can't explain to him."

"And what is that?" she asked me softly.

"We've both been hurt and have lived through things that maybe others wouldn't understand."

"And you do?"

"Yes…no? Oh, I don't know, but when I'm around him, even though our first encounter was everything *but* what I had imagined-"

"You feel normal?"

Then tears started to flow, and I couldn't stop them as Mother pulled me into a hug.

I truly didn't care if he was scarred. I saw beyond that; to a man who was more than his battle wounds. Wounds that saved his country, and I saw that last night when he spoke of his brother and father. The games he played growing up, and the fond memories of running the halls. Halls that I would hopefully be filled with our own children one day.

He was so kind and treated me like any other woman, not a burden to be taken care of. Not that my mother or brother, even though at times it felt like that, treated me that way. He asked about my interest and seemed genuinely interested in what I had to say.

"Then be the future queen I know you to be. Do not give them one second to doubt you. You go in there with your head held high. Do not let the gossip of the court tear you down. You show King Rollan you are a prize worth catching."

"Am I?"

"Worth more than gold. Any woman can strut their feathers, but not many have a heart like you do, and I believe he knows that."

"You do?"

"I know so, darling."

I hugged her tightly, "thank you, Mother."

She returned my embrace, then stepped back from me, guiding my arm to hook onto hers.

"Now, let's go before Fredrick sends the guards."

I laughed, "he would, too!"

"Don't remind me," she scoffed, playfully mocking my brother's overly protective ways.

"Actually…" she continued, "I have an idea…"

CHAPTER 14

ROLLAN

The whole court was eagerly awaiting to see what princess had agreed to marry me. I watched the doors, waiting for Princess Ellenora to be announced, ignoring all the whispers and gossip going on around me. I was on edge, wondering what they would say when they saw the Princess was blind. I didn't want her under any scrutiny when she would be their queen. They would show her the respect she deserved, and I had a plan to make it so.

My heart stilled as I saw the doors open, but my position didn't allow me to see her, to my great annoyance.

The ballroom went silent in anticipation, and I could barely breathe as they announced the queen and her daughter.

I watched as they entered the room, and my heart started to pound with how beautiful the Princess looked. She wore a cream-colored gown with pastel pink on the sleeves and bodice. Her hair was up in a soft, artistic bun, with loose curls framing her face and crown to show her rank. She glided with such grace, her head held high, daring any courtier to mock her. Gasps filled the air, and many glanced from her to me, and I could see their minds working.

Then whispered words were spoken that made my stomach clench, and my chest tighten.

"Is she blind…the poor dear…is she being forced into marriage…lucky for her, at least she won't have to look at him…"

I turned to my advisor, who was waiting with me, and he gave me a nod of encouragement.

"Show them you are King and that she is a worthy Queen."

I nodded, then made my way toward the princess, the crowd parting for me, all eyes on me and the beautiful woman before me, who, in such little time, had snuck her way into my heart.

I stopped before them and bowed, "Welcome, your Majesty and Princess Ellenora. I am honored to have you here tonight."

They bowed in return. "The Honor is ours, your Majesty," Ellen spoke confidently, but I noticed she was nervous.

I could feel every gaze in the room watching, waiting to see what I would do next.

"May I have the first dance, Princess? I hear you are quite light on your feet," I leaned close and whispered.

She smiled widely, and I couldn't help but give her my own.

"Learning all my secrets?" She teased as she held out her hand for me to take, which I took and tucked into my arm as I led her to the dance floor. Jeren told me about many of her accomplishments when I was worried about the ball and her not being able to see and found out she was a marvelous dancer.

"I hope to uncover them all," I responded with all seriousness. How different I was from just a few days ago. I wanted to know everything about the beautiful girl before me, and I prayed I would have all the time to do so.

"But what is a lady without her secrets?"

I pulled her into my arms, "I hope there are no secrets between us."

She pulled back, and I was wondering if I was too forward, and I mentally kicked myself. I never wanted to make her uncomfortable, but I didn't have time to apologize before the music started. Which I was grateful for. Otherwise, my guest might think something was wrong, and a false rumor might start. I positioned her hands and guided her into the waltz.

We glided effortlessly across the floor to the music and something changed within me. I never enjoyed dancing, but now I wanted to dance with this woman all night. I watched her expression, and I wanted to know if she thought the same thing. Did she enjoy dancing with me as much as I enjoyed dancing with her?

"What is going on in that mind of yours," I asked her eagerly.

"I'm just grateful I have an actual dance partner who is *not* an instructor or my brother."

"You mean, you have never danced with another man before?" I was shocked.

"No. My brother, though I love him, is very protective of me and…" she paused, and I twirled us around before encouraging her to keep going.

"My castle is like a prison in some ways. He fears rejection on my behalf, and so only the instructor and he were allowed to dance with me."

"In a way, I'm grateful," I told her.

"What do you mean?"

"That means you have no other man to compare me to, and now I have the privilege to be your first dance and…" I paused, hesitant. "Hopefully, your last."

She glowed at my words, and I wanted to bend down and kiss those beautiful lips, but I refrained myself. We hadn't even announced if there was going to be a marital alliance, but I knew I would do everything to make it so.

"I look forward to it," she responded with crimson cheeks that made my hands ache to touch.

I twirled her around, and when I brought her back to the starting position, I pulled her even closer. This desire to be near her was getting stronger the more we glided across the floor.

The music started to slow, but I was far from done being in her arms. "Would you oblige me with another dance, Princess?"

She was breathless but agreed. "And please, call me Ellen."

Her permission broke another barrier that was leading me toward my ultimate goal of having her as my wife. And it wasn't just because I needed a queen or an heir. It was her.

All of her.

"Rollan," I responded.

"Rollan," she smiled, and my name on her lips did something to my heart that I knew I could never recover from. At this point, I was willing to beg her brother for an alliance to keep her in my life. I shook my head, wondering where this lovesick fool came from, but I couldn't help but enjoy the change. I used to mock those who were acting just like me, and now I didn't have a care in the world.

The whole ballroom was drowned out, and it felt as if it was just her and I dancing in each other's arms.

Our second dance started to close as the music slowed and softened. I was reluctant to let her go, but I couldn't dare ask for another dance.

"Would you like a drink?" I asked her. That way, we could socialize, and I'd have an excuse to return to her and stay by her side while we caught our breath.

The music started up again for another dance, and I started to lead her away, but she seemed hesitant.

"Is everything okay?"

"Yes, I…" she looked down shyly, "would I be too intrusive to ask for another dance? I'm having so much- Oh!"

I scooped her up in my arms and led her into the dance. How could I say *no*? It was exactly what I wanted to do, anyway.

I pulled her close, grateful it was another couple's dance and not a quadrille. I didn't want to share her with anyone at the moment, and I daresay that no one would probably want to link arms with their king and go in a circle. They were all scared of me.

But not her.

This beautiful woman who chose me. Who was gracious enough to give me a second chance when I didn't deserve it.

"Thank you, your Majesty, for obliging me."

"Rollan," I corrected her, wanting, no needing, the familiarity between us.

She smiled, "Rollan," she spoke my name in a reverent whisper that made my chest swell.

I bent towards her, "it is my pleasure, Princess." Hoping she could hear the sincerity in my voice.

The music started to slow again, and I insisted on resting before taking her back to the queen while I went to get refreshments for us.

"I'll be right back," I gently squeezed her hand before leaving her with her mother, "but I promise we'll dance again." She gifted me with another smile before I made my way to the punch bowl, but my name was called out about halfway there, and I turned to see who it was and saw Lord Ellra only a few feet away.

"Your Majesty," he bowed as I turned to face him fully, wondering what he needed. He was one of the Lords who had jurisdiction over the lower half of my Kingdom, but I didn't want to talk politics tonight, not when I had more important things to worry about, like winning the affections of my Kingdom's *hopefully* future Queen, but when I noticed Lord Kern and Lord Bewer were with him, I inwardly groaned. Every time I had a council meeting with any of the Lords who had jurisdiction over my lands, Lord Kern and Lord Bewer always made things difficult. I almost wished I hadn't left the princess. I would be stuck with these men until they told me what they wanted and demanded I fix it, but they would be disappointed tonight. I was not in the mood to entertain their petty pleas to raise taxes or change laws that would be more detrimental than good. In fact, these men were the few reasons I stayed King. I would not let my Lords ruin my country over a few extra coins. I may look abhorrent, but I was no savage. Even if some of my Kingdom could not look beyond my scars, I knew that the few good men and women who worked the mines and farms were the backbone of my Kingdom, and I would not put more burdens on them than necessary.

"Your majesty," Lord Ellra bowed, then slightly turned to motion to the other men. "We would like to congratulate you on the alliance that you are forging with the Kingdom of Kendall."

"Thank you," I nodded, then turned to leave, hoping that was all he had to say, but a hand stopped me.

I looked down at my arm, then up at Lord Ellra, giving him a glare to let him know he had crossed a line. He quickly took his hand off of me and cleared his throat.

"We…as a Lord on your council, I wanted to ask if it was wise to marry someone who…"

"Who is what?" I asked with a stern voice, daring him to speak the words. "Beautiful? Enchanting? More fit to be Queen than any other women I have yet to meet."

"Well, yes, she is all those things, but…" he stumbled around his words."

Then Lord Brewer stepped up. The tall skinny man, who reminded me of a snake. "What Lord Ellra is trying to say is that we are worried that because she cannot see, that she may not be the best fit for our kingdom."

My anger flared, and my fist clenched at my sides. I was holding myself back by a thread.

"And it isn't just us who think it. Many-"

"Who? Name them," I seethed.

"Well…I…"

I stepped forward and spoke in a deadly but calm voice, "I will have *no one* speaking ill about our future Queen," I snarled, "She is more qualified to rule than most of my Lords." I emphasized the words, and they became uncomfortable. Good.

I didn't even excuse myself but turned away from them as rage burned through me as I made my way back to the Princess. I would take us away from this stuffy ballroom and order some lemonade. I didn't want to be around these judgmental people anymore.

Then, I stopped short. Memories of our first meeting flashed in my mind, and guilt filled me.

Was I no better than those conceited men?

I vowed right then that I would prove to her with every fiber of my being that I was not like the Lords of my Kingdom and protect her from them at all costs.

I continued my way, not making eye contact with anyone until I found her talking with Jeren. I was surprised her mother and brother were nowhere to be found, but grateful since her brother and I were still on fragile ground.

"Ah, Your Majesty," My advisor spoke out loud for the Princess's sake, and a new appreciation for him swelled within me. I would find a way of thanking him for putting Ellen in my life.

I gently grabbed her hand, and she turned towards me but spoke to Jeren. "See that some lemonade is sent to my study for the Princess and myself. I'm through with this ball,"

He nodded, and I turned to lead her away, but she slightly pulled back. Turning back to her, I saw her face was full of worry, and I wanted to brush my hands on her cheeks to soothe her, but I knew that was too intimate for the middle of the ballroom.

"What's wrong, Rollan?" she asked quietly, then a mischievous grin came to her lips, "I thought you were having a wonderful time dancing with me, but now I know it was false modesty," she feigned a sigh, and I couldn't help but smile, but it didn't last after the thought of what happened to me flashed in my mind.

"It's not that. I just need a break." A break from all the gossip and to protect her from the cruelty of my court. I could handle it, but I couldn't handle them belittling her.

She stepped closer, almost bumping into me, and her hands slowly felt their way up my arms before settling on my shoulders.

"If we leave now, then they win."

"Excuse me?"

"I may be blind, but I am not deaf. I know why you want to leave, but I refuse to back down and leaving will only prove to them how weak they think their future queen is…your queen."

I couldn't breathe at her words. How badly I wanted her to be my queen, and it seemed she wanted it too, but already I was receiving backlash from an alliance that may not even happen.

"Together, we are strong, Rollan. Let us prove to them that we are a force to be reckoned with. That we don't let our past define us, but that we let it make us stronger."

"And how do you suppose we do that?" I couldn't keep the defeat from my voice.

"You'll see soon enough."

The words of courage that came out of her lips made me want to press mine to them. I've never met a braver person in all of my life.

"Princess?"

I turned to see her brother making her way towards us. We slightly acknowledged each other before a scowl came to his face. He looked between his sister and me, pinching his lips. That's when I noticed how close his sister and I were.

I should have taken a step back, but I didn't. Instead, I grinned and moved a little bit closer.

He cleared his throat and Ellen turned towards him.

"It's ready, Ellen."

She smiled, then glided her hand down from my shoulders to pat my chest gently, and a shock of pleasure went through me from her touch. "It's going to be okay. Come and see."

Then her brother took her hand and guided her away from me, and I followed, wondering what she was up to. I also wanted to keep her close in case any more Lords approached me.

King Fredrick guided her to the dais, and I noticed her harp was in the middle of the raised platform.

I watched as her brother guided her to her seat next to the large instrument, my heart pounding with anticipation as the ballroom quieted and everyone started to make their way over to see what the blind princess was going to do.

She took a big breath, and I wished she could see the look of encouragement I was giving her.

Then she played.

It wasn't the music that pulled me to her a few days ago. It was nothing like you could quite imagine.

Her fingers flowed across the harp in an effortless manner, making a sound as if heaven itself opened up and angels were singing.

She played from the heart. Only someone with a soul as beautiful as hers could play such a masterpiece.

The whole room was enchanted as everyone held their breath, listening to the music that pulled at their very own heartstrings.

It was then that I knew I loved her.

It wasn't just any love. It stirred something so deep within my soul, that it shook me to my very core.

I loved Ellen, and I would love her forever, and I would marry her with her brother's approval or not.

She slowed down, her fingers moving in a lullaby, and I noticed many courtiers swaying as if under her spell. The same spell she pulled me under.

Then, all too soon, she was done.

An ear splitting applause erupted in the ballroom. I looked around and realized her tactic had worked.

She had won the hearts of my kingdom, just as she had won mine.

CHAPTER 15

ELLEN

I slowly put my hands in my lap. The applause made my heart swell with pride. Mother was right; I just needed to show them, and I did. She suggested the idea right before we left for the ball, and I hesitantly agreed. Then, when Rollan wanted to escape, I knew I had to follow through.

It wasn't just for me, but for us.

I waited for my brother to come and escort me back to Rollan but was pleasantly surprised when another King's voice spoke next to me.

"That was breathtakingly beautiful, Princess," Rollan said in awe, and I lifted up my hand for him to take so he could guide me back down the dais, but when his lips gently pressed to my skin, I couldn't move since flutters erupted in my stomach and coursed through my whole body.

How I wished to know what he looked like. To see his gaze that I could so vividly feel on me all the time.

"What's wrong?" he asked, and I must not have schooled my expressions like I had thought.

"Nothing, just nerves."

"Come, you must be parched, and I owe you some punch. I'll also have you know that there are Lords lined up to dance with you after that performance."

"Really?"

"Yes, but they shall just have to wait because their King is going to dance with you first, and frankly, they don't deserve to be in your presence."

He said the last part with a slightly irritated tone, and I wondered what had happened in the time we had been away from each other, but I decided not to ask and ruin the moment. I've heard enough with my own ears, but hopefully, my performance changed their thoughts about me.

He gently squeezed my hand, then hooked it through his arm as he led me down the dias and across the dance floor to get some punch, the feeling again of wishing how I could see him. I know he was called the scarred king, but to me, he was so much more.

We stopped several times to greet people, and by the time we got our punch, two songs had already passed.

"Ellen?" Rollan whispered close to my ear, making my skin tingle.

"Yes?" I spoke breathlessly.

"I know I promised you a dance, but..."

I knew what he wanted, since I wanted it as well.

"I would love to get away."

Without another word, I was pressed to his side as he guided me out of the ballroom.

"I'm using a servant's door, so we don't have to talk to anyone."

"Brilliant! Where are we going?"

"My study."

While I wanted to be alone with him, we both were still unmarried and as a princess, I had to keep my reputation intact, even if he was the man I was hoping would be my future husband. Not that I didn't trust him, but we worked so hard to win over his court today and didn't want rumors starting. It was already going to seem strange that we left the ball.

"It's not that I don't trust you, but I'll need a chaperone."

"Drat! You're right." Then he paused, "wait here."

He let go of me, and I stood there in the darkness by myself, hoping no one was around. I knew I would look foolish just standing here alone, but I realized I didn't have to worry since the pounding of footsteps told me he was already returning to me.

"I'm back. Sorry, I should have taken you. I guess I'm still getting used to-"

"Don't worry. I was fine," I assured him right as he wrapped his arm around my waist, holding onto my hand as he guided me. I loved being so close to him even though my every nerve was on end.

"I grabbed the first maid I could find," He said slightly out of breath, letting me know he ran to grab a chaperone. I couldn't help but smile as his eagerness met my own.

"Thank you, Rollan."

He quickly guided me around the castle, and I took a mental note to start learning the layout of the castle so I wouldn't be so vulnerable. While I gave up on learning before, tonight proved otherwise.

Then he quickly stopped, and I tried not to stumble forward, but failed, and I was grateful he pulled me back, right against his hard chest.

"Forgive me."

But I just laughed. We were both so nervous that we were stumbling down the hallway like drunken fools.

"You're fine," I squeaked out, being closer to him than before.

Now that we had stopped, the tension started to grow as I tried to catch my breath.

The sound of a door opening made my heart race, and he led me inside. After a few moments of walking about my knee bumped into something.

"Please sit," he told me and softly guided me to the seat. Then I felt his weight next to mine and realized we must be on a sofa.

"Can you please fetch the princess some lemonade?" He called to the maid. I could hear her footsteps soften.

"Wait, what about my chaperone? Should we ask someone else?"

"Why? Are you planning to sabotage me?" his voice teased.

"No, but…"

"Do you trust me?"

"I do," I told him truthfully. Even though I barely knew him, I trusted him completely.

"Don't worry, she'll be back before anyone notices."

I smiled. In actuality, I liked our time alone.

Then it hit me; we were *alone*.

I'd never been alone with a man before, not that I thought he would do anything untoward, but my confidence started to wave.

"You played beautifully tonight," he told me, breaking the silence, and my words gushed out of my mouth in response.

"Thank you. I've always wanted to play, and even though I lost my eyesight, my mother still encouraged me to fulfill that dream."

He chuckled, and my hands were engulfed in his. "Are you as nervous as I am?"

I swallowed, giving a slight nod. I was less nervous playing in front of his entire court than sitting with the man who could possibly be my future husband, but it was assuring that he was nervous as well.

"What a wonderful ally to have on your side," he told me.

I took a breath, but it soon left me as he started to rub circles with his thumb on my hands. I swallowed the lump in my throat before responding.

"Yes, she has always encouraged me not to let anything hold me back from living my life to the fullest."

"I wish my mother was here to do the same. She died when I was young. Maybe I wouldn't have made so many reckless decisions if she was still alive."

"I'm sorry. I don't know what I would do without my Mother. I'd be lost for sure since my Father died when I was an infant."

It was a moment before he responded.

"Your father was a good man from what I knew."

"You knew him?" Shocked at his response.

"I met him when I was seven when my father went to discuss opening trading routes between your kingdom and ours. I believe the queen, your mother, was pregnant with you at the time." Then he chuckled. "You're marrying an old man, Ellen.

He cleared his throat, "that is if you'll still have me?"

My chest swelled, "I've never wanted anything more in my life."

"Really?" he sounded doubtful.

"Yes."

"I know we started off on the wrong foot," he started to apologize again, "but I will spend the rest of my life proving to you that my love is strong and true. That I'm not marrying you because I have to but because I want to. I would have chosen you again and again. No other woman lives up to your beauty, both inside and out."

"Really?" it was my turn to ask. "Even though I am blind?" I had to ask, even though I knew the answer.

He gently grabbed my face in his hands, and I held my breath. I was slightly disappointed when our foreheads touched, but I was also grateful. I've never kissed a man before, or any male for that matter.

"Out of everyone I know, you are truly the one who sees. You look at the heart, and I'll forever be grateful that you looked past my pride and chose to stay."

He brushed this thumb along my cheeks, and I eagerly wanted to do the same to him.

"Rollan?" I asked hesitantly, a question on my lips that was burning to get out.

"Yes, Ellen," he responded quietly, his breath caressing my face.

"May I do something?"

He didn't respond, and I worried about what he might be thinking.

"May I...may I touch your face?"

Heavy tension filled the room, and I knew I crossed a line.

"I'm afraid you will not like what you feel," I could hear the heartache and anguish in his words, along with fear, but he had nothing to fear from me, and I wanted to prove that to him.

I leaned forward, hoping I wasn't too close, but wishing I was. "Let me be the one to decide that."

Then I slowly raised my hands and reached out to him, but he must have pulled back since my fingers grasped air. Embarrassment filled me. I shouldn't have pushed him. I put my hands back down, but they were suddenly captured by his strong hands once more. Suddenly, his lips touched my palms as he kissed each hand with such tenderness.

"Please, don't judge me," his voice was full of anguish as he guided both of my hands to his cheeks. His whole body stiffened as if to await judgment.

I held back a gasp, but not from disgust… but from the pain he had suffered alone. The left side was smooth, while the right had a jagged skin that ran from the middle of his lower jaw all the way to his eye. I traced my finger along the scar.

"Does it hurt?" My voice trembled with sympathy.

"No," he stated with no emotion.

I traced my thumbs along his nose, and up to his eyebrows, running my fingers along the arch of each brow, then back down to his lips, where I traced them with my fingers. They were full, and I was tempted to lean forward and place my lips on his in a gentle kiss, but I held back.

Then I ran my hands along his jaw, past his scar, and to his hairline. I ran my fingers through his thick hair that ended at his shoulders.

"What color is your hair?" I asked.

"Black," he stated breathlessly, and that's when I noticed the pounding of his heart. I hoped it was because he enjoyed my touch and not from fear. I continued my exploration of his face, trying to piece the image of him in my mind. I made my way back to his eyes.

"And your eyes?"

"Blue."

"Blue," I stated softly. "like the sea, or a summer's day?"

"More like a storm."

I smiled at his description, then traced his scar once more, and he tensed.

"Please don't. From what I can tell, you are very handsome..." He scoffed and pulled back from my hands, my fingers ached to continue touching him. I hated how he didn't believe me.

"Why do you doubt me? Because I cannot see? Let me assure you that those men and women are nothing compared to you."

"You give me too much grace, Princess."

"Ellen."

Then I reached out my hands and prayed he would take them, and was happy he brought them back to his face, so I could touch him once more.

"How did it happen?" I asked softly.

He took a big breath as if living the memory, "when the mountain men came to war with us, I fought alongside my father and brother. When my brother was struck down, I ran to him but was ambushed by a soldier behind a tree. My father came to my rescue, and because of that, he died saving my life. They both did."

I had no words. Sorry wasn't enough for what he had lost. He truly was alone in the world, and his scars only reminded him of what he had lost.

I leaned forward, taking my arms and wrapping it around his neck in an embrace.

He pulled me to him, clinging onto me as if his life depended on it, but I enjoyed the closeness.

"I'm so sorry, Rollan. I know I cannot bring them back, but I am here to share your pain. I'm not just an alliance, but your friend."

He pulled me closer to his chest, and I could hear his heart pound and wondered if he could hear mine as well.

"Oh, Ellen, you are much more than that to me."

Then he pulled back and whispered into my ear, "may I…may I kiss you?"

I gave a slight nod, and suddenly my lips were captured by his. My heart practically pounded out of my chest as I eagerly returned his kiss. With my arms already wrapped around his neck, I pulled him closer.

"Your lemonade, your majesty," came a maid's high-pitched voice, and I pushed back with a gasp.

Rollan's laughter filled the air, and I thought it was anything but funny. I touched my hair to see if anything was out of place as embarrassment filled me.

He grabbed my hand, "you look beautiful," then he put our hands down between us and started rubbing circles with his thumb on my palm again as I heard the maid pour the lemonade.

"That will do," Rollan told her and soon her footsteps faded, along with the door being shut.

"Here." He placed a teacup in my hand, and I drank deeply from it, anything to distract me from what had just happened.

"Did the maid leave?"

"Yes," his voice was soothing, and I relaxed a little, even though I knew it wasn't proper for us to be alone. "Don't worry, the thought of what your brother would do to me if I ruined your reputation, is more than enough."

I laughed this time. "Thank goodness for brothers."

He grumbled, "Yes."

I knew they were at odds, but I prayed they would soon see past their differences for the sake of the alliance.

"May I ask you something?"

"Of course. I don't want any secrets between us." I wondered if he was going to ask how I became blind.

"May I touch your face?"

Oh.

I smiled and put down the cup at his words, and faced him.

He took my cup from my hand and I heard the clank, letting me know he set it down.

Then gently, with fingers that were calloused from sword training, but were welcomed on my skin, he moved along my jaw, until he cupped my cheeks. It was different this time from when he cupped my cheeks before. His thumbs ran along my eyebrows, and I relished in his touch.

I knew what was coming before he said anything.

He ran his thumbs gently over my eyes, "What happened?"

"It was a fire."

"In your room?"

"No," then I became hesitant, and his hands left my face, and I wanted to put them back.

"If it's too painful to tell, I understand. Some scars go deep."

I carefully reached for his hands and was grateful he placed them in mine and did just as he had done to me and placed them back on my cheeks.

"The story involves more than just me, and with how you feel about a certain someone, I would hate to cause any more rift between you two."

"Your brother?"

"Yes, but it wasn't his fault," I quickly interjected. I didn't need another reason from Rollan to hate my brother when the tension between them was already high, but I wanted to share my story. He was vulnerable in sharing his, and I wanted him to know mine.

"I understand and will try to listen to your story without judgment."

"Thank you," grateful he was willing to listen.

I paused to gather my courage."

"Not many know the exact story because I don't want others to blame Fredrick. While they know my blindness was caused by a stable fire, they don't know who started it; besides my mother and myself. Mother wanted to protect him as future King, and I wanted to protect him because he's my brother."

I paused to see how he would react, but he squeezed my hand to continue instead of responding.

"When I was younger, my brother was fascinated with horses, and my father had just bought a new mare. One of a kind. Well, she arrived late in the night, and even though my father warned my brother to wait until he was there to go and see the mare since her temperament was wild, my brother disregarded his words and snuck out one night to the stables. His footsteps in the hallway woke me up. I followed him to the stables and hid behind a stall to see what kind of trouble he was getting himself into.

He heard footsteps outside, and in a panic of worrying he would get caught, he dropped the lantern he was carrying and accidentally started a fire. He didn't know I had followed him, and he left the stables without me to go get help. I tried unlocking the latch to the stall, but it wouldn't budge. The smoke grew heavy, and I started to scream and cry, begging him to come back and save me. He did, but it was too late. The damage was done to my eyes, and I've been blind ever since."

"Is that why you were hesitant when we went to the stables?"

"Yes," hoping he didn't think me incapable.

"I wish I would have known. I'm sorry." His tone was full of regret.

"Don't be. You didn't know."

"Are you also afraid of horses, now?"

"No, in fact, I used to love riding, but ever since that day, I'm afraid it's been far out of reach."

He paused, "what if it wasn't?"

"I don't understand?" Wondering what idea he was thinking of.

Suddenly, we were interrupted by footsteps making their way down the hall. One pair I knew, the sound being etched in my brain since forever.

"Fredrick is coming," I rushed to say, moving as far down the couch as I could before the door burst open.

"There you are! I've been looking everywhere for you. Do you know the gossip you are going to cause? I thought Maren had more tact than that, but it seems their king doesn't."

"And I thought the King of Kendall would have more propriety and manners, but you seem to do what you wish with no thought of others or the King you are visiting," Rollan interrupted him and I could feel the couch move, letting me know he stood up.

"Others? My sister is blind and needs protecting."
Fredrick's footsteps coming closer.

"And more capable than what you give her credit
for!" Rollan snapped back.

My heart swelled at his defense of me. He didn't think
me weak, even after I told him my story.

"You think I don't know that!"

"No, from what I see, you hold her back."

"How dare you speak to me that way. You will-"

"Fredrick, that is quiet enough! Rollan made sure
there was a chaperone here with us." I interjected before he
said something that would ruin this alliance.

"Rollan? We haven't even drawn up the alliance, and
you are already speaking his given name? And where is this
maid? All I see are you two!"

"Now dear, settle down," I heard my Mother from the
doorway. "I told you, they were fine."

I was so glad she came. Fists might have gone flying
if she didn't come.

"Why don't you go back to the ballroom, and I'll
finish up here," she told my brother patiently.

"Mother, they-"

She must have given him a look because the next thing I heard, he was grumbling under his breath along with the sounds of boots stomping out of the room.

"Don't mind him. He's on edge with other matters, but I will say it would be best to either retire for the night or head back to the ballroom."

I didn't want to face the stuffy faces and comments of the court again, so I dismissed myself for the night.

Rollan's hand gently grabbed mine as he helped me stand and led me to my mother where she hooked her arm through mine.

"Goodnight, Rollan," I told him.

"Goodnight, Princess. May you sleep well."

I counted the footsteps to the door and heard Mother twist the handle.

"Your Majesty," came Rollan's voice from behind us and Mother slightly turned and I moved with her, wondering what he was going to say. "I want to move forward with the alliance and marry your daughter, but I am worried your son will not agree."

His confession made my heart soar, and I eagerly waited to see what my mother would say.

"Do not worry about my son. He'll come around."

"I love her," he told her bluntly, and I couldn't help the gasp that left my lips.

He *loved* me?

His confession mirrored my own feelings, but I was too shocked to respond. I wasn't expecting love from this alliance, but I couldn't help but be thrilled that he felt something for me besides an arranged agreement, even if the feelings were fresh and new.

"I know," Mother told him matter-of-factly before she guided me out the door without another word.

CHAPTER 16

ROLLAN

I couldn't keep my gaze off of her as I watched her leave, my heart still pounding from our interaction, and soon I was alone with my thoughts.

I turned to where she sat on the sofa, brought my hand up to my face, and touched my scar. The scar she did not tremble from in terror. Her touch still lingered, burning a hole all through my body, making me feel things I had never felt before.

I closed my eyes, reliving what had just happened. I was so worried she would run away, just as every other Lady I have been acquainted with had, but she didn't. She touched me with such gentleness as I waited for her reaction, but all I could see was genuine concern for me, especially when I told her my story of how I received my scars and hearing hers in return. It now made sense why the King was so protective of his sister. It was probably the guilt he felt for his part in Ellen becoming blind. I couldn't blame the man, especially now that I understood why.

I also never felt so vulnerable in my life than in that moment when the words spilled between us. Our hearts connected in a way that I didn't know how to explain.

Then that kiss. Her lips were so soft against mine. My lips burned just thinking about it, and I brushed my finger over them before running them through my hair.

I let out a deep and content sigh.

She was perfect in every way, and I couldn't wait to make her mine, which led me to confess to the Queen how I felt about her daughter, hoping she would tell her son. I was prepared to do anything to win Fredrick over, if just to have Ellen in my life. I watched her reaction when I spoke the feelings of my heart, and even though she didn't respond, the smile she wore told me that she felt the same way, but I knew I would still ask her tomorrow.

Tomorrow.

When it was just us.

It was getting late, and even though the ball was still going on, I only wanted to head to my quarters and dream of Ellen. I got up and headed for the door. Enough time had passed that she probably was in her room and sound asleep.

I opened the door and stopped when I saw the man who was the only barrier to our love waiting across the hall. He was leaning against the wall with his arms folded, and my defenses went up.

I quickly checked myself. My pride almost made me lose her once, and I wouldn't make that mistake again. If he were here to cut off our agreement, I would remind him that he promised me three months, and I was going to hold him to that. Maybe to persuade him, I would give him a more negotiable price for trading our precious ore and metals with his kingdom. I wasn't one to grovel, but I would do anything at this point to keep Ellen in my life.

I stepped forward, words ready on my tongue, but he raised his hand to stop me. I waited, watching him and wondering what he was going to say.

"You care for her, don't you?" His voice was monotone, but I could hear a hint of skepticism.

I was surprised at his words when I was expecting a battle.

"Yes. I love her." I responded quickly. I didn't want him to doubt me; if I had hesitated, I knew he would have.

He said nothing, but his gaze told me he didn't believe me.

"What about when we first arrived?" His eyebrows raised, challenging me. His voice was even, and accusing.

His blow hurt, and my gut clenched. I wished I could take back that day and start over.

"I was a fool."

He grunted as if agreeing with me.

"But can't even fools redeem themselves?" I offered.

He still didn't say anything, and we stared at each other for a while.

Then he stepped towards me, and I straightened to my full height letting him know I was also a King, He was in my Kingdom, and wouldn't back down. That I truly did love her and would fight for her.

He stopped and looked me over. Then after what seemed like ages, he gave me a nod and turned, walking back down the hall.

I watched until he turned the corner, releasing a breath I didn't realize I was holding.

He didn't deny me, but I was still unsure what his nod meant. All I knew was that he gave me another chance, and I wouldn't ruin it this time.

CHAPTER 17

ELLEN

I heard shuffling around my room, and it stirred me awake.

"Sophia?" I called out. My body was still tired from the night's events. Not to mention the difficulty of trying to fall asleep when all my senses were on fire as I replayed the kiss over and over in my mind.

"Sorry to wake you, Princess, but the King wanted you up and ready before the sunrise?"

"What could Fredrick possibly want that couldn't wait."

"Actually," she sounded hesitant, "It was King Rollan who told me to make sure you were ready."

I sat up quickly and pushed the covers back, excitement coursing through me. "Really? Did he tell you why?"

"He says it's a surprise, but to wear something warm."

I made my way to the edge of the bed, "well, let us hurry then, shall we."

She quickly got me dressed and put my hair in a stylish but tight bun. The whole time, my anticipation grew, but I didn't say anything. I knew Sophia was hurrying as fast as she could. Soon, I was out the door being led to where the King wanted me. Thinking of him brought a blush to my cheeks. Last night we shared so much, and that kiss was a dream come true. He was so respectful when he asked me, not just assuming I wanted it, especially when I wasn't able to see his expressions that would usually hint at one wanting to be kissed...or give a kiss.

I let out a content sigh. Everything was finally going as planned.

I heard a door open and a cool breeze hit my face. "Are we outside?"

"Yes, we are to meet him at the stables."

I stopped and pulled her back to me, "the stables?" I couldn't keep the worry out of my voice. He knew I was afraid of the stables? Was he hoping to help me overcome my fear? I didn't know if it would work, especially if something were to happen; I wouldn't be able to get myself out without seeing.

"Don't worry, Princess, not inside."

I swallowed my fear before gently squeezing her arm to let her continue, but she didn't move. Instead, I felt her shift beside me.

"Ellen," a deep voice spoke my name, and my fear was forgotten as footsteps came towards me.

"Thank you. I'll take her from here," Rollan told my maid.

"Yes, Your Majesty."

My arm was soon engulfed by his. I was more aware of him than ever. The kiss that happened between us changed everything.

I wondered if we would kiss again.

I swallowed the lump in my throat thinking about it, and mentally shook my mind to clear those thoughts. I needed to focus on the task at hand.

"Come," he told me, and slowly led me down the stairs. "Ten more steps."

"Thank you, Rollan." His awareness and kindness towards me really showed me that he cared.

He paused, and I could feel him slightly turn towards me. Then his hand was on my cheek, his fingers brushing down and gently grabbing my chin. I couldn't stop the blush that engulfed my whole body. Was he going to kiss me again? Right here in the open?

"I assure you, it is my pleasure," he whispered softly, so close to me that I could feel his breath on my cheeks, making my own breath stop in anticipation.

Then he suddenly dropped his hand and cleared his throat, and I wondered if others were around us.

"Ten steps?" I asked to break the tension, and a small chuckle rumbled through his chest."

"Yes," he said, and I could hear the smile in his voice.

When we made it to the bottom, he guided me to the right.

"My maid said we would meet you at the stables, but didn't say exactly what we had planned?"

"We're going on a ride."

"A ride?" My voice quaked with anxiety. "On a horse?"

While I knew that might be the objective of today's outing, hearing it made my body clamp up. The last time I had ridden was before the accident.

He stopped and grabbed my hands, "do you think I would ever let anything happen to you?"

I shook my head, but fear coursed through me anyway. It's not that I didn't trust him. I just didn't know if I had enough courage to give him that trust. At least in this regard.

"Come," he was walking again, "I'd like you to meet my horse."

I heard a horse neigh relatively close, and I tugged Rollan to a stop. My fear was not letting me go any further.

"Don't worry, we're not riding him just yet. I want him to smell your hand and know your scent. Then we'll go from there."

I still hesitated.

He turned me to him and pulled me into an embrace. "Let me help you, Ellen. Like you have helped me."

"Helped you?" I asked, confused.

"More than you'll ever know," he whispered in my ear, then softly kissed my cheek, making me forget all about my fears.

He took my hand and guided it out until I touched soft fur.

"This is Bruner, my steed."

"Hello, Bruner," I said quietly, and the horse shook.

"He can sense your fear. Relax, he won't hurt you," Rollan assured me.

I took a deep breath to calm myself.

"There. See, you're doing great," he stepped up directly behind me, closing any distance between us as he guided my fingers over the horse's muzzle.

"What color is he?" I asked, trying to distract myself from how close he was to me.

"He's black with white hooves and a white star in the middle of his forehead."

"He sounds beautiful."

"He's magnificent." I could hear the pride in his voice and his love for this animal.

"And the horse I'll…" I gulped, "I'll be riding?"

He chuckled, but I couldn't find anything humorous, "my dear sweet, Ellen. You'll be riding with me. He's more than strong enough to carry us both."

Before I could reject, his hands were on my waist, and I was lifted into the air. A squeal left my mouth as I was placed on the saddle, his hands guiding mine to the horn.

"Wait! I don't know about this!" I told him. "I thought you said we would go slow. Maybe we can ride tomorrow?"

"And miss out on a beautiful day like this? Not a chance. We'll go as slow as you want. I promise. Now, hold on tight," he exclaimed, and the saddle jerked to the side. I held on for dear life, but it was only a split second since he quickly wrapped his hands around my waist, securing me to his chest.

"Are you ready?" he asked in my ear.

"No!" I squeaked out, and it just wasn't because I was on a horse. No, it was because a powerful and strong man, whom I so happened to have just met, but had strong feelings for, was holding me tightly against his chest.

He laughed at my exclamation and gently squeezed my middle to assure me that everything was going to be okay.

I felt him nudge the horse's sides, and the large steed started to move forward. I tensed up for only a moment, but not long after the familiar feeling of swaying from side to side brought back the thrill that I used to love, and my fears left me.

"See, I told you I would never let anything happen to you."

I leaned my head back against his chest. "Thank you, Rollan. After the accident, I never thought I would be on a horse again."

"As long as you are with me, I'll make sure you experience life to its fullest."

My heart swelled at his words, which held so much weight for me. I wanted to experience everything, and I knew I could do that as long as I was with him.

I relaxed and let myself enjoy the ride. No one was here to tell me no, or restrict me in my heart's desires. I truly felt free, and it was all because of him.

We stayed like that for a while until my curiosity got the better of me.

"Where are we going?" I eagerly asked.

"To a special place not too far from here."

I decided not to pry and let him have his surprise. We fell into a comfortable silence from the horse's movements.

The sounds of gravel turned into the crunching of leaves, and I became curious.

"Can you describe the scenery to me?"

"I would love to. We are in the forest that is next to my castle. The trees are turning color for the upcoming season.", "but the prettiest scenery is right in front of me.

I blushed at his description.

"And…" I asked, trying to distract myself.

"I see a couple of Blue jays up ahead, and a few squirrels."

Then he leaned close, his breath right next to my ear, sending a flush to my cheeks, "but the most beautiful thing I see is right in front of me."

I ducked my head at his compliment.

"Ellen…"

"Yes?"

"I meant what I said yesterday."

His voice was earnest, and I knew exactly what he was talking about. It gave me the courage to confess my feelings as well.

"I love you, too, Rollan."

I didn't realize how stiff he was until he let out a breath at my words.

Then his hand was gently on my jaw, tipping it up and back to face him. I tilted to the side, his arm securing me to him, so I wouldn't fall.

"I am never letting you go," he whispered, and I knew it wasn't just about the hold he had on me now. Then his lips were on mine once more, and I returned his kiss with eagerness, my hands reaching up and gliding into his hair, while the other hand wrapped around his neck.

Bruner let out a sound of agreement while shaking his head. We pulled apart and laughed at the horse's perfect timing and theatrics.

"Did I mention he is also an excellent chaperone?"

"It's probably for the best," I laughed once more.

Then I could feel him stiffen once more.

I placed my hand on his chest, "what's wrong?" Fear crept in my voice. Was he having second thoughts?

He took another deep breath, "It's your brother. I don't know if he'll agree to this. He's been against it from the start."

"I know, and for that I apologize. He'll come around," I told him, praying it was true. Fredrick was so protective and stubborn.

"I hope so, because I'm about this close to marrying you without his consent."

"And start a war?" I joked.

"I would start a war, if it meant that you were in my life," he spoke with all seriousness, but I would never let him do that. While I wanted him with all my heart, I knew my duty to my kingdom came first.

"Let me talk to him. I'm sure by now my mother has talked some sense into him."

"I'm serious, Ellen. I can't lose you," his voice pained.

I traced my hand up his chest until I cupped his cheek. "You won't," I assured him.

But instead of responding, he brushed his face along my palm until his lips touched my fingers, and he gave me a gentle kiss, then grabbed my hand and gave it a gentle squeeze before bringing it back down to my lap, where he didn't let me go.

"We're almost there," he told me as I leaned back into the comfort of his arms.

We rode in companionable silence for about ten more minutes until a familiar sound reached my ears.

"Are we near a waterfall?" I asked after the sound of rushing water filled my ears.

"Yes," he sounded excited now. "When I was a boy, I used to come here with my brother and fish. There is a waterfall to the right that is about as high as the castle ceilings. While I know you won't be able to see it, it's special to me, and I wanted to share it with you."

I gave his hand a squeeze to let him know that I understood what a sacred place this was to him, and it meant a lot to me that he was sharing something so close to him with me. It probably brought back lots of memories that were both painful and memorable, just like the stables were for me.

"Thank you for sharing this with me," I told him, and he responded with a gentle squeeze to my waist.

He pulled on the reins, and Bruner stopped.

"I'll get down first, then help you."

The saddle wobbled as he hopped off. Then his hands were firmly around my waist as he slowly put me on the ground, and soon I was locked between him and his horse.

"You are so beautiful, Ellen. Inside and out," his voice came out gruff and full of emotion.

Tension was thick, and I thought he would kiss me again, but instead, he grabbed my hand and led the way. I was slightly disappointed, but after his words, I knew he was probably resisting since we were alone.

"We'll walk slowly since it can be slippery, but there are some large boulders we can sit on, and I'll describe the scenery to you."

He guided me around the rocky ground and helped me sit on a large boulder before taking his place next to me.

CHAPTER 18

ROLLAN

I haven't been back here for years. The memories were painful, but for some reason, having Ellen here with me, this place felt different this time. As if I could heal from my past and all that has happened.

I had a future to look forward to now. One filled with a beautiful and caring girl by my side. Something I never thought would happen.

I looked at her once more as she tilted her head slightly back, taking in all the sounds around her. She was breathtaking, and I had to keep resisting the urge to kiss her. I already kissed her once, when I promised I wouldn't while we were alone, but she called to me, and I longed for her.

She tilted her head slightly to me.

"What are you thinking about?"

"Nothing," I quickly responded, and she laughed.

"I feel so free being here with you," she told me with a smile and a sigh. "Content and carefree, and I don't wish it to end."

"It won't. I'll take you here as often as you want," I promised her.

She smiled and it lit up her face, but when I glanced at her eyes that were blind to the world around her, an ache went to my chest. How I wished she could see the beautiful scenery before her. Yet, she was still happy. It both humbled and intrigued me.

"How can you not be angry at the world, or your brother from what happened?"

She stiffened. No doubt I had surprised her with the question, but I had to know, but I prayed I didn't ruin our moment together.

She folded her hands in her lap and closed her eyes.

"I've learned long ago that you can't change your past, but you can be optimistic for the future. It wasn't my brother's fault I snuck out. Sure, I could blame him, but then we would both be miserable and if you haven't noticed, he still holds a lot of guilt for what happened that night. I don't need to add to his burden. With the help of my mother, I decided that I wouldn't let my blindness stop me. I would live life to the fullest and with her help I have…to an extent."

"I admire you, Ellen," I reached for her hands. "I hope that one day I can heal like you have."

"You can," she told me with confidence. "It takes time, but I'll be here for you every step of the way."

Her words stirred something in me, as if I was healing already.

"Now," she smiled, "let's take a walk to that waterfall. I want to feel it on my fingers since I can't see it."

I hesitated, "I'm not sure that it is safe. The slope is steep, and only one person can go at a time."

She raised her brows. "Today I rode a horse when I thought I never would. I trust you, Rollan."

I stood up, her confidence in me overrode any fear I initially had. I couldn't deny her anything. "Then let's go."

I grabbed her hands and carefully guided her along the river, telling her where to step.

"The slope is about five steps ahead. I'll have you go first while I'll hold onto you and tell you where to step."

"Sounds perfect."

Once we were right in front of the trail that led to the waterfall, I started to give her instructions.

"Okay, step with your right foot first, and I'll push you up."

She followed my directions precisely, but when she slipped, my heart about jumped out of my chest in fear.

"We should go back. I don't think this is a good idea," I yelled over the sound of the waterfall.

She grinned, "we'll be fine. Aren't we almost there?"

"Yes, but…"

She took a step forward, and I could only follow.

It took twice as long, but we finally made it to a rocky ledge that was right next to the waterfall.

"It's so loud," she yelled at me, and I could only grin as water sprayed on both of us.

"Reach out your hand," I hollered back.

She slowly reached out and a gasp left her lips as her fingers touched the pounding water.

Then a laugh that was so pure and full of joy filled the air.

"It's remarkable," she spoke almost breathlessly, then leaned forward to run her hands through the waterfall once more.

I watched her, locking away with memory forever.

"Come, this path also leads behind the waterfall."

I went around her to lead the way, my hand on her back to keep her stable.

Once I found my footing, I turned to grab her hand to follow me.

She started to step towards me, and right as her foot touched the ground, the rock under her shoe slipped to the side, making her lose her balance. My hands desperately reached out to grab her and pull her to safety, but they slipped past her fingers, which were wet from touching the waterfall.

"Ellen," I cried as I desperately grabbed for her again, but it was no use since I slipped forward as well, making us both plummet into the waterfall.

The weight of the water crashed down on us, forcing me to release her from my arms. I screamed out her name, bringing water to my lungs, and I closed my mouth, forcing myself to focus. I had to save Ellen. I couldn't lose her like I've lost everything in my life. I was a fool to bring her here. I kicked hard against the pounding current.

Once I reached the surface, I choked out the water from my lungs while looking desperately for the girl who had changed my whole world, and what I saw made me cry out in anguish.

I swam my hardest to her body that was face down in the water. I scooped her up in my arms, carried her to the river bank, and laid her on the rocky shore.

"Please!" I sobbed, shaking her shoulders to wake her up. Praying this was just a nightmare. When she didn't respond, I started to push down on her chest, hoping to get the water out of her body. Something I learned when training for war.

"Bruner! Bruner!" I yelled for my horse. I needed to get her back to the castle as quickly as possible and to my healers.

I heard his hooves and ran to meet him, throwing Ellen over the saddle, before hopping on. Once I got her situated in my arms, I nudged my steed, pushing him into a gallop.

Tears blurred my eyes as we raced back. "Please, don't go. Please, come back to me."

The last time I cried was when I lost my father and brother, but nothing compared to the pain and anguish I felt now.

I choked on a sob, and my whole body shook. The only light in my life was truly being taken away from me.

"I need you."

CHAPTER 19

ELLEN

My head pulsed, and a moan left my lips as pain coursed through my entire body. The last thing I remember was going on a ride with Rollan, but that wouldn't explain why I hurt so much.

"Oh, darling, you're awake!" my mother cried next to me, "Sophia, grab the healer, and make quick about it! Tell him the princess is finally awake!"

I heard the shuffling of my handmaiden's feet, and the door open and close.

"Mother, what's going on? What happened?" My voice was barely recognizable with how strained it sounded.

"Oh, darling, do you not remember?"

I closed my eyes and laid back down on the pillow. The faint, blurry light I could see was making my headache worse.

"You fell…"

"Fell?"

"From a waterfall," her voice choked up.

Memories flashed back quickly of Rollan taking me on a horseback ride and him leading me up to the waterfall. I was careless and wanted to touch the water again and leaned forward when I should not have moved as he told me to do.

I wasn't the only one who fell.

"Where's Rollan? Is he okay?" My voice is surprisingly strong.

"He's just fine dear. He brought you back, and you've been unconscious for two days now, and…"

I reached out a hand and felt around until I touched her. "It's okay, Mother. I'm alive."

Her hand was soon brushing my hair back and cupping my face. "We were sick with worry. We thought we had lost you."

Suddenly we were interrupted by voices hollering in the hallway.

"You will not see my sister!"

"You will not tell me who I can and cannot see in my own castle! Step aside, King Fredrick!"

"No! You think she wants to see you after how careless you've been. She almost died because of you.

The alliance is off. We are leaving tomorrow! I can't believe how foolish I was to even agree to this nonsense!"

I tried to call out, but my voice was faint. It wasn't Rollan's fault. If Fredrick knew it was an accident, he wouldn't be saying those mindless threats.

"Then leave! We don't need your alliance anyway."

My heart stopped at Rollan's words, wondering if I had misheard, but the way Mother stiffened, I knew I had not.

I waited for him to take back his words, to say he didn't mean it. That he still wanted the alliance.

After what had happened between us. Did he not really mean what he had said?

I couldn't breathe as I waited, but his next words confirmed it.

"Why you even came in the first place is beyond me," Rollan snarled.

"It's settled then," Fredrick shot back.

Tears escaped my cheeks and I pushed up and tried to get out of bed.

"What are you doing? You need to rest." My mother tried to push me back gently, but I resisted.

"No, I can't let Fredrick ruin this."

I fumbled out of bed, but I had no energy and fell to my knees.

"Rollan!" I called from the floor, "Fredrick, please don't do this! It wasn't his fault!"

I could feel Mother next to me. Her hand slipped around my waist to help me pull up, but I didn't want to go back to bed, I wanted to run after the man who just broke my heart and demand if he meant those words. To demand he put up a fight.

"It's no use darling. Fredrick's mind is made up, and there is no use changing it. They've been at it for a while now, but anything King Rollan says falls on deaf ears."

"No, it can't be true. It was an accident, Mother. It wasn't his fault. I didn't listen when he told me to stay put."

"I know, darling, but maybe it's for the best." Her calm voice only irritated me more. What happened to letting me choose my own life? I felt like everything was slipping through my fingers and I couldn't stop it.

"The best?" I asked, bewildered. "How can leaving be for the best? I love him, Mother, and he loves me."

"How can he love you when he was careless," came my brother's voice, and my body burned with anger.

"You ruined it! You ruined everything!" I cried. "Get out!"

He quickly disregarded me. "Calm down, Ellen. I am saving you from a man who does not treat you as you deserve."

"And you do? You look me up as if I am some fragile flower, but I am stronger than that. My blindness does not mean I am weak! I am strong and more capable than you think. So, don't you dare tell me what you think is good or not good enough for me, because you are wrong!"

It felt so good to tell him the words of my heart.

"It doesn't matter. We are leaving tomorrow morning." His tone spoke of finality.

"No."

"I don't have time for this." His voice annoyed and I heard him leave, and for some reason, I knew this wasn't just about the incident.

"I've forgiven you," I called out to him, and I heard his footsteps stop.

"What?"

"I hope that one day you can forgive yourself for what happened to me. I've forgiven you, but it seems that you still need to forgive yourself. You feel that protecting me is the best way to do that, but you're mistaken. You are holding me back and holding yourself back from living life to the fullest."

There was no response. The tension thick in the air as my words hang between us. Then footsteps sounded, along with the closing of the door.

I leaned into my Mother's arms.

And cried.

CHAPTER 20

ROLLAN

I heard her call my name, and regret instantly filled me for saying those words she no doubt heard. I would do anything for an alliance with her, but the only obstacle between us was standing directly in front of me.

"Leave," he hissed low, no doubt keeping it quiet so his sister wouldn't hear.

I stepped forward, and he reached for his sword that was on his side. I could easily beat him, but the cries I heard from inside stopped me as they twisted my heart with anguish. I wanted to burst in there and comfort her while apologizing for being the fool that I was. Telling her that I didn't mean the words I said and only said them out of anger.

Fredrick started to pull his sword out. I didn't want to fight him. The only reason was I knew it would break Ellen's heart, and I would not make Ellen suffer more because of my pride, even though I wanted to start a war with the man before me, but that would not bring me Ellen, only more pain and suffering...which would make me lose her in the end.

Which is why I would let him live.

"You will be gone by tomorrow morning. Don't ever set foot in my Kingdom again, or war will be at *your* doorsteps."

If I couldn't have her, then I couldn't risk the chance of seeing her. It was too painful already. I needed to make this a clean-cut. Otherwise, we would both suffer with the what-ifs.

"Fine."

At his response, I turned and left, and it was the hardest thing I ever had to walk away from in my life.

-The story continues with The King's Maid.

Made in the USA
Columbia, SC
19 January 2026

78155420R00098